C

Learning
to Love It

SEVEN STORIES & A NOVELLA

THOMAS FARBER

CAPRA PRESS
SANTA BARBARA

For Hsu Yin Peh and Hsu Li

❀

Copyright © 1993 by Thomas Farber.
Printed in the United States of America.
All rights reserved.

"Learning to Love It" first appeared in *North American Review.*
"Public Anatomy" first appeared in *Manoa.*

Typography by the Pagination Station.
Printed by McNaughton & Gunn.

LIBRARY OF CONGRESS CATALOGING-IN-PUBLICATION DATA

Farber, Thomas, 1944-
Learning to love it : seven stories and a novella / Thomas Farber.
p. cm.
Contents: Learning to love it – To be eaten with a spoon – A land of men & women too –
Citizen Mad Dog – Zenobia – The one you're with –Song of the self-made – Public anatomy.
ISBN 0-88496-368-3 : $10.95
1. Boston (Mass.) – Fiction. 2. San Francisco (Calif.) – Fiction.
I. Title.
PS3556.A64L4 1993

813'.54 – dc20   93-17837
                                                   CIP

CAPRA PRESS
Post Office Box 2068
Santa Barbara, CA 93120

(Distributed to the trade by Consortium Book Sales, 1045 Westgate Dr., St. Paul, MN 55114)

"My formula for the greatness of a human being is *amor fati* : that one wants nothing to be different, not forward, not backward, not in all eternity. Not merely bear what is necessary, still less conceal it . . . but love it."

—Nietzsche, *Ecce Homo*

"When a person has sex, they're not just having it with that partner. They're having it with everybody that partner has had it with for the past ten years."

—U.S. Health and Human Services Secretary Otis Brown, 1987

PART I

Learning to Love It

*R*AY WAS A GREAT athlete in high school and college. Massachusetts schoolboy record for the high hurdles. Star shortstop. AA and AAA minor league ball before knee injuries ended his career at twenty-four. Then two packs a day and enough beers to take the edge off, this plus an insistent refusal to reminisce about the glory days not simply with semi-strangers but even with close friends. Ray did, however, take into the future several imperatives from what had been the passion of his life: bend your knees; keep your eye on the ball; always be moving forward.

Ray often said he'd die young—"Who cares, I'm going to die young anyway," was how he usually put it. This verbal tic stemmed from an assortment of impulses and insights: from self-reproach for the smoking and drinking; from an attempt at a reverse curse, in effect asking God to give him a break since Ray was taking the risk of saying God wouldn't; from a simple reading of the medical odds; from a weakness for the maudlin; and from what proved to be a quite accurate bone marrow intuition about his fate. Also, Ray was driven by a genuine if intermittent desire to be free of all that bound him. Think of him as the first male in his family since the great-

10

grandfather from County Kerry not to fight in a war in the U. S. Army: baseball injuries spared him Vietnam. Think of him as the first male in family memory to hold a job in peacetime, go to college, to stay this side of alcoholism, not to take the occasional swing at his wife. All this despite his father, Ray I (Ray himself being Ray Jr., his own first-born being Ray III). A father who, unemployed with spouse working two jobs, had the capacity to watch Ray compete in the high hurdles as a high school sophomore and then tell Ray he'd shamed him by finishing second. When the drunk teenage driver's van hit Ray's car, therefore, there was irony—in high school, Ray often drove while half in the bag—and for Ray at least some element of relief. His parents imposed a Catholic funeral on his wife, who was in shock, his unemployed cousin lying by arguing that Ray had only recently talked about wanting to start going to Mass again. When the funeral procession left the church in Charlestown, the line of mourners' cars became separated from the hearses and limousines, took a wrong turn on the Southeast Expressway, and never did arrive at the gravesite. Keep your eye on the ball, Ray might have said, suppressing what kids in New England continue to call a shit-eating grin.

Ray, married with two children, in his late thirties, one more blue Monday heading for work in downtown Boston. Another gray December morning, cloud ceiling low. At Park Street Station, off the T and up the ancient escalator—out of order yet again, so hustling up two steps at a time, trying to beat his previous personal best. A guy coming down the stairs past him wearing a kelly-green sports coat with brass nautical buttons. "Jesus, Mary, and Joseph," Ray says to himself, "does nothing ever change?" And then mutters, "Screw it, I have no problem with that."

Off the escalator onto Tremont Street, past Bailey's, where his grandmother once worked serving ice cream sundaes to

Brahmin matrons. Tan cloth raincoat, hod-carrier's cap, black rubbers over penny loafers, tweed sports coat, regimental tie, gray slacks. Camouflage. Protective coloration. In this environment, absolutely ordinary. The coat and tie an effort to mask the rapaciousness of the species, Ray often thought, watching proceedings over at the State House. The legislators, that band of male primates, distance between rhetoric and reality rivaling *Animal Farm*. Ray's own costume belied, or made irrelevant, by the speed at which he walked. He couldn't help it. In the office he'd go from cubicle to cubicle at an incredible pace, arriving at someone's desk like a skater braking to a halt—*whoosh*—just in front of the goal. He'd do this perhaps twenty times a day. Or he'd finish a meeting at another agency's building and walk—churn—back to the office with members of his staff struggling to keep up. "Bend your knees," he'd tell them, though they always received the line with a slightly puzzled look, having no reason to read it as metaphor, and though it wasn't fair anyway, since Ray's fuel was anxiety, of which he had so much that he'd arrive at the office not only not winded but soothed.

Ray's bag lunch, peanut butter and jelly sandwiches he made for himself each morning at five thirty. In by seven, long before his employees. Reading the *Globe,* having the first of maybe fifteen cups of coffee. Then out for another to one of the croissant shops proliferating in the downtown, though the idea that croissants were so saleable in Boston drove him crazy. *"Buy American,"* he used to mutter—growl—as he stood waiting for change.

Lunch was usually at 11:40, once a week over at the Fatted Calf, a burger and beer joint for politicos and lobbyists at the foot of Beacon Hill, hard by the government offices. Conspiracy stories. Political gossip. Ratio of men to women 9:1. Ray eating his burger, generally the first person in, waitresses still gearing up, and then heading back to his office at a ferocious clip, shooting a glance at King's Chapel as he turned right onto

Tremont, tooling past the Old Granary Burial Ground, Park Street Church, cop on horseback, Salvation Army bellringers. Maybe having another lunch around three, pulling out the paper bag from home.

Sometimes, feeling all he'd done was create yet another bureaucracy, one more indispensable layer of civil service workfare for people like himself, after leaving the office Ray would head over to the Museum Bar on Huntington Ave. It always made him laugh: right up the road from the Museum of Fine Arts and Symphony Hall, just a joint with its hookers and street alcoholics of various races and ethnicities, equal opportunity and affirmative action in action, cabbies and dispatchers between shifts from the garage around the corner, booths along the wall with roaches to whack, floor of the men's room flooded, somebody passed out with his head on the bar, no hassles, nobody giving a shit—no one unmasked, exposed— all this with a mural depicting some South Seas paradise on the rear wall. So Ray would be there—"Anybody's lookin' for me, I'm over at the Museum," he'd call to the night desk man as he went out the door, the guy just nodding, leaving Ray to wonder—putting away a beer, another, another, eating dozens of crunchy orange goldfish, all salt and 'cheese-flavored', until finally the thought of even one more made him sick, often not getting home until nine, nine-thirty, driving through the sleet, wipers clacking, prying off his rubbers on the back porch, dinner cold on the table, boys already down, Barbara not saying anything but making him feel bad.

One of the things that disturbed Ray was Miss C, as he called her. C for Cabot. When she first came to work for him he was just starting out and she was already eligible for Social Security. Driving a hard bargain and proud of it, he offered her eighty a week to be executive secretary. Soon she pretty much ran the place. Wrote most of the grants, the annual report, hired, fired. After a while he raised her salary to one fifty, but more than that she wouldn't take. The deal was, he realized, she wanted somewhere to be.

Every day, accompanied by her border collie, she came in from Hyde Park on the T. About five one, eighty-five pounds soaking wet. (Ray tried not to picture her naked). Pure will. Never sick, incredibly sharp. A spinster, had perhaps never been kissed. Her mother married a Brahmin, whose family, appalled that his bride was Irish, cut him off completely. Then her father's business went under and he began to drink, finally disappeared. Miss C—Emmie to her mother—took a job while still in high school, and soon the routine was that she worked while her mother stayed home. At the end of the day Emmie would return, having also gone shopping, to make dinner for both of them, and then she'd wash up. Her mother kept her from dating, which perhaps suited Emmie: men seemed only coarse to her. ("I've never really understood what kind of beauty artists see in the proportions of the male nude," she once said to Ray.) This, in any case, is how things went until she was nearly sixty-five, when her mother died. Miss C thought then that she too would die, but when she didn't she bought the border collie and got in the habit of walking it every morning in Arnold Arboretum. That first April after her mother was gone she watched spring come in: crocus through the late snow; witch-hazel; some early tulips; forsythia, jonquils, daffodils. Not long after, she applied for the job with Ray, the proximate cause being that her old boss got angry because she bought a Chrysler. "You don't need a Chrysler," he shouted, knowing that she rode the T, that she never went anywhere. It infuriated the man, all of it, including that she'd saved money on the pittance he paid her. So she took a job with Ray. Which was fine with him, given her extraordinary competence and loyalty, but on the other hand she seemed too typical an aspect of the city, another life shaped by denial, loss, sacrifice to family/prejudice/economic exploitation. Ray didn't really believe revolutions would change the world—the first thing he'd noticed about Castro was a brother well up in the hierarchy—but perhaps, he'd think, hearing Miss C in the next office, perhaps a revolution might be worth a try.

One time Ray arrived at Miss C's house to visit—she was seventy-five by then—as she was coming down the ladder after putting up the old wood storm windows. Later she cooked a full dinner for the dog, pot roast/lima beans/mashed potato. Another time Ray came out, Miss C was down on all fours cutting the back lawn with hand clippers. She cackled: "The lawnmower's broken." He used to wait for her to complain, but she wouldn't. That is, he waited for her to complain about her fate, as opposed to tirades about this employee or that one, but she never did, even when the surgeon decided to amputate a breast though she'd been in perfect health her whole life, even though the surgeon later conceded the growth was benign. Miss C's only real problem, it seemed, was who to will her house to, but then she found an organization that pledged to care for her border collie until its death if she left adequate resources. Ray had it checked out—Miss C had gone through a period of getting burned by contractors, benefitted from three new roofs in three years—but everything seemed for real.

The kid who killed Ray. He came around the curve on the wrong side of the road. No suprise: he'd been drinking Scotches straight up at a local bar for more than an hour. O'Malley. Twenty-four, unemployed, a mother who couldn't say no. Her van. He attended Suffolk University for a semester, then quit to work for an uncle at Wonderland, the dog track out in Revere. Liked both uppers and downers. Liked to bet the spread against the Celtics/Sox/Patriots. A would-be bully who'd never moved out of the family home. A type utterly familiar to Ray, so that if at the moment of the crash he beheld death's visage, saw the kid through the two dirty windshields, Ray would have had to laugh. Nothing more exotic than another thwarted local loser? Merely the naked face of home-grown violence? The New England fan equivalent of skin-heads out at NFL games in Foxboro if you were black and made the mistake of needing to go to the men's room; the umpteenth teenager to smash your car window to get the tape deck while your car was parked illegally when you went to the movies and decided to risk the ticket to save being gouged at the garage; or that representative of the lumpenproletariat in Dorchester who smoked angel dust and then ripped the face off an eighty-year-old for her wedding ring. Going on to serve a life sentence, all of it pointless except maybe for the fee to the court-appointed lawyer, salaries of the judge/bailiff/cop/stenographer/guard/warden/counselor/parole officer.

Being good. Ray was good in part because he was afraid not to be, afraid he'd become an alcoholic, be unemployed, be like his father/grandfather/great-grandfather. Beyond this, Ray thought that whatever Dionysius spoke for in other cultures, in Boston the god spoke not for freedom but for mayhem. Child abusers; tax-evaders; politicians fixing a deal with contractors, hospital walls crumbling; State Police cheating on promotion exams; star guard fixing the basketball game; victory being not joy but tearing down goal-posts. Those with means moving out to the suburbs, then deploring urban violence.

Car windows. A friend put a sign in her Honda: *No Radio.* Came out one morning to find the windshield smashed, a different sign taped to the dashboard: *Get One.*

Ray did cut loose, once, right after leaving baseball. This was in '69, the whole world going crazy. He went to Europe, read books on the beach in Italy, smoked hash, thought he might just figure out how to stay a while. He knew a little of the history of the continent, it seemed nothing if not a record of war after war, one population being exterminated, yet another springing up in its place, the castles were fortresses, all this was clear. Nonetheless, in Italy for some reason Ray could imagine a middle ground, there governments seemed the danger, individuals and clans endowed with an instinct for peace, for savoring, nurturing. But in Boston, Ray felt, in Boston you really had to choose which side you were on.

One night he was out with his old friend Brian, drifting down Exeter Street. He and Brian played ball together in grammar school and high school. Baseball had saved Brian from two alcoholic parents, especially from a father who liked to beat the shit out of him. Now, a gambler and occasional coke dealer, Brian was drinking heavily. As they passed one of the fern-bar singles places, Brian saw a guy playing Asteroids by the window, pushed his way through the crowds at the door, walked up to him, and said, "I want to play," which the man correctly understood to translate as, "Get out of my way," to which he responded, "Fuck you," after which Brian took a swing, so Ray tried to ride his back to slow him down. Hard to do, since Brian was a bull. In fact, Brian once said to Ray's wife, "What fucks like a bull and winks?" and then winked.

The next day, Brian hung-over and sober, Ray asked, "What was that about?"

"Come on," Brian said, "the guy was just another Carolan or Hoolihan or whatever. I didn't like his attitude. Tryin' to be a fuckin' preppy or something. Thinkin' his shit doesn't stink. Fuck him." The accent on 'fuck', not 'him.'

Being good. Ray was good to his wife Barbara because he knew her, because he felt gratitude, because he felt obligation, because she was an extraordinary person—bright, giving, beautiful, loyal—because he was afraid of the wider world—AIDS increasingly crossed his mind as an argument for monogamy—because she put up with him, because he loved her even though he was certain that to love is to coerce. As for the kids, Ray was good to them because he couldn't help it, because when he first held Ray III in his arms he experienced a hormonal change, felt himself in that instant an utterly different person. Juices reconstituted, as he put it to himself, grinning. This was beyond choice: he just wasn't about about to let anything hurt his child. A sensation that only deepened as he watched Ray III grow with an openness and trust that amazed him. Sitting in the rocking chair in the living room one night, studying his infant son, it occurred to Ray that he'd had to teach himself everything, everything. He'd been lonely all through his childhood, a very, very long time. Tears came to his eyes; he shook his head. Maudlin while sober, he thought. And envying my boy. Pathetic. What's become of me? He wiped his eyes, inspected Ray III's diaper. "A bean's a bean," he then said to his son, "but a pee's a relief."

When Ray returned from Italy—Barbara wrote that if he didn't come home soon she'd start dating other guys—he took a job working for a church-sponsored recreation program in Roxbury helping inner-city kids. That is, housing-project blacks. Ray did so well the board encouraged him to set up a halfway house for ex-convicts, and he did so well with that that soon he had two halfway houses and fifteen employees not to mention a roster of pacifist volunteers doing alternative service. His system then began to attract notice because it had no therapy. Non-therapy, Ray called it, that is, nothing more than job counseling, use of existing social services, a place to stay, and a few rules to offer some structure during the transition from prison. Remarkably effective without any talk of rebuilding the soul of the convict, not to mention consonant with Ray's skepticism: no unnecessary assumptions. Please.

There were only two problems for Ray. First, as the organization grew his salary grew, and as his salary grew he kept thinking he was overpaid; and second, his fear that the whole network might fold and he'd be unemployable. After all, what he had was a B.A. and some expertise on the baseball diamond. Barbara would say, "Fine, you want security, go work for the State Department of Corrections, Department of Youth

Services, whatever," but they both knew he wouldn't. This though she shared Ray's amazement that a career line could be built out of so little. So it was that despite praise from people in the human services community, Ray felt he was doing it with smoke and mirrors. Wasn't it just common sense, really? To hold all this together, he came in at seven, left at seven, brought paperwork home for the weekends: the only way he could carry it off.

Actually, sometimes Ray knew he had special gifts. Blarney, for instance, being able to bullshit people, set them at ease. He and all the kids he knew growing up could do it, but out in the world it was apparently a scarce commodity. Then too he understood loyalty, or, loyalty was for him not an ethical imperative but, rather, like being able to play the ball on the short hop, something he didn't remember learning. So Ray was constantly surprising people by his loyalty, which, briefly, kept him surprised. As for the ex-cons, they were dazzled by freedom, which they failed to comprehend in all its complexity, coming as they were from the intricacies of not-freedom, and in part they saw Ray as responsible for their freedom, though he never claimed such power. Beyond this, Ray had no need to dominate the men, simply talked in practical language about the choices available to them. Perhaps too they sensed Ray wasn't physically afraid. He was, actually, if he thought about it, of course some one nut was capable of going crazy and pulling a gun. But day-to-day, because the men often had less self-control than other people they seemed to Ray refreshingly direct, not nearly so menacing as some bureaucrats he'd encountered.

If the ex-cons were street-smart but not educated, Ray found his staff overeducated but not smart. Which was fine, since it left him some place to operate out of. Further, many of his employees, even the ones older than he was, seemed to need a father, would place him in that role whether or not he wanted to be there. That's just the way it was.

Barbara. Considering everything she could have been worse
off. They'd bought the house when the market was still down;
now it was worth a fortune. More, to everyone's suprise Ray
had actually acted on his words about dying young and taken
out a big life insurance policy.

These practicalities aside, Barbara had the benefit of not
wishing she'd just had one last chance to talk to Ray. They'd
known each other fifteen years, had been married for ten.
They were best friends, long since familiar with each other's
sorrows. Often he'd wake her in the middle of the night.
"Babs, I can't sleep," he'd say mournfully, and, now wide
awake, she'd console them both.

Barbara failed to wish she had one more chance to talk to
Ray even though he didn't really speak to her the last six
months before the accident. His silence—except for the absolutely necessary words—began after Ray III, age two and a
half, came home from the hospital. It was a miracle, what the
surgeons had done, but as Barbara saw it Ray was irreparably
altered, finally just shut her out.

The nightmare started after Ray III had a cold for several
days, but then instead of recovering kept vomiting, began to
seem increasingly unresponsive. At the hospital, delirious, he
was taken to Intensive Care. "Now we know what we're
dealing with," the doctor finally told them after the blood test.
"The high level of ammonia in the blood is diagnostic. This
syndrome is rare, and poorly understood. Not genetic; usually
comes after a viral infection. There's swelling in the brain, so
we're going to begin medication to reduce it."

The next morning Ray III was still comatose. "What we
have to do now," the surgeon told them, "is check the spinal
fluid pressure so we can determine just how much medication
can be safely used." The surgeon seemed to be planning to
leave it at that, but Ray insisted on knowing more. "All right,"
the surgeon replied impatiently. "I understand. Informed con-
sent. Well, we use a bone saw to remove a section in the skull,

making a kind of window, then cut through the membrane below, the dura mater, after which we guide an ICP monitor to the ventricle of the brain to measure intracranial pressure."

This alone could have sent Ray over the edge, Barbara believed, but the surgeon, apparently feeling Ray had goaded him, wasn't finished. "If the swelling continues, the medicine isn't working. What happens then is the liver continues to turn to fat, and the brain swells until the brain stem, which controls breathing, is pushed through the bottom of the skull. This— herniation—is terminal. If the medicine does work, however, we operate again to take out the monitor and replace the bone square. There'll be no anesthesia when we begin, since your son is in coma and feeling no pain."

It was too much for Ray, Barbara thought. Not that he'd been great even at her deliveries. "I gotta go now," he kept saying when she was in labor, and he'd head out for yet another cigarette. He just didn't know how she could stand it. But with Ray III, he crossed into some other zone completely. Perhaps, Barbara thought, perhaps because for weeks after the miracle of Ray III's survival, scar slowly disappearing as hair grew back, Ray III had terrible nightmares. The staff in Intensive Care restricted his movement and bound his wrists in gauze to keep the bandages from being disturbed, which appeared to explain why after he came home you could see him in a yet another dream wringing his hands, moaning, shifting, trying to escape. Nor would he cry: perhaps from his point of view he'd cried at the hospital, and all that had happened was someone then came and hurt him again.

Ray knew it was wrong, he felt terrible guilt, but even so he stopped talking to his wife. The deal they'd made, Ray seemed to be saying, was that he'd work and she'd raise the children. *Protect them,* he'd apparently understood that to mean. So he turned on Barbara, something he'd never done before. Emotionally spent after the operation, getting almost no sleep for weeks because of Ray III's nightmares, she decided to wait

until spring to talk to Ray about it. But then he was killed. The
short-term effect was that life became easier, his anger now
absent. Nor did she have to deal with his insomnia/fear of
being found out/anxiety about money/tirades about nepotism
and patronage. His reflexive or genetic need to establish some
security, his rage at being vulnerable to such a need.

A few months before the kid killed him Ray suffered the
paralysis of one side of his face. "An aberrant response of the
immune system to a viral infection," the specialist explained,
"always affecting just the right or left seventh cranial nerve."
Not life-threatening, but also there was no treatment. The
paralysis almost always ended, eighty percent of the time
within several months. Ray badgered the man. Was it stress?
Smoking? Diet? In fact he wasn't about to change his life, but
he did want some explanation. "Listen," the specialist replied.
"It's just random. No cause, no blame, no nothing. Not something you did or didn't do. The nervous system—the brain—
tells itself a story about whatever it encounters, which is to
say, it looks for a pattern. But this phenomenon has none. Not
everybody gets this viral infection, and of those who do, only
a very small number get this paralysis. The impulse of the
nervous system to find order is its nature, but in this kind of
situation such an impulse just cannot be successful."

As for the level at which the phenomenon could be described if in no way instrumentally affected by the capacity to
describe it, one side of Ray's face retained its mobility while
the other was unable to move. Along with hyper-acusis, that
is, increased sensitivity to sound, which only made Ray's
insomnia more frequent and severe, and beyond the fact that
he had to tape his eye closed at night to protect the cornea
since the lower lid sagged, and after you noted that his forehead was furrowed on only one side, the paralysis gave his
smile an odd quality, a kind of wryness even when Ray was
most happy, one corner of his mouth drooping slightly, and

also endowed even his scowl with an adjoining neutrality. So it was that when the kid's van barrelled around the curve on Ray's side of the road, when he saw it coming right at him, Ray began to grimace and was saying to himself, "I know Babs understands why I've been hurting her," and thinking, "We really don't need any more time to set it straight," and wondering if the new corrections grant would come through from the Feds and whether Miss C would be all right and Jesus, Mary, and Joseph, who's going to be there to teach the boys how to play the game, and even at the moment of impact—"Always be moving forward," were Ray's last words to himself—he also appeared to be sporting some kind of a grin.

* * *

To Be Eaten
With A Spoon

"*H*EY, KNOW WHAT YOU call a guy with both legs chopped off? *Neil.*" This is Vincent speaking. Laughing, out of control, fighting to stop laughing. Finally able to continue. "Hey, did you hear about the leper who said to the prostitute, 'That's OK, keep the tip.' "

Vincent: fifteen in 1986, fourth of five children, hardworking student, bad acne, not athletic. Shy and insecure except with friends—all male—with whom he's razor-tongued. Half-hearted born-again Christian looking for someone to love at Bible Study classes, acute sense of himself as a too-familiar type. Too scared to invite any girls out. Articulating this fear in his diary, with underlining, as "1. *Wanting to be accepted for who I am as a person . . .*" Enormous yearnings for sex and he knows not what, the interminable meantime assuaged by comic books, horror movies, texts on adolescent psychology, and extensive reading on monsters/extra-terrestrial life/the Bermuda Triangle/sharks/killer bees.

Horror films: "hack and slash." *The Exorcist, The Thing, Halloween, Alien, Prom Night, Friday the 13th, Dawn of the Dead, Creepshow, Mother's Day, Phantasm, Eraserhead,*

Nightmare on Elm Street. Generally there for the double bill. Once in the theatre, adrenalin secreting, both scared and excited, Vincent's again in a world where his courage passes the test. As for the sight of what's monstrous, growing or shrinking or utterly out of control: well, he can relate. Much of it either resonating with what he fears about his own hungers or what he imagines will be the effect of these hungers on the first available other.

So horror films for Vincent, yes, but not just any movie with blood and guts: an aficionado, he wants his horror well-crafted, and desires not only the experience but comment on it. To this end he suscribes to *Fangoria*, a magazine which reviews horror movies, covers films in production, and dis-cusses how they are made, its tone alternately straightforward and tongue-in-cheek. *Fangoria* also has a personals column in the back, ads free for subscribers.

After much thought, Vincent places his: "Pen pals who like horror or fantasy, females preferred, age 15-25. Please send photo." Checking the mailbox each day for two weeks—his father has to remind him there's no delivery on Sundays—he's disbelieving when the first letter arrives. "Dear Vincent: Hi! How are you? I'm doing ok, myself. How's school/work? Got to go. Love you madly. Cindy."

Novice at this though he is, Vincent realizes that such art is little better than his present life, but at the same time he can see possibilities, if only in the "love you madly." Writing several long paragraphs back to Cindy, encouraging her by example, he then waits another twelve days for her response. In this note, barely longer than the last, Cindy says she's passing his name on in a "friendship book." Which, he learns, consists of several small pieces of paper stapled together, the maker sending it off to one of his own penpals who sends it to someone and so on and on until the book is full of names and addresses and mailed to the beneficiary. Typical entry: "I like

Kiss, Spandau Ballet, Boy George, and Stephen King. Ans. All." The return addresses include Louisville, Brooklyn, Pontiac, St. Paul, Chico, and La Mesa.

Vincent immediately begins a spate of correspondence, and soon the letters start to pour in. This is work, however: many people don't reply, take weeks to answer, or, like Cindy, send brief notes, preferring to be written to than to write. Worse, Vincent learns that you can begin a correspondence with someone and then without warning they stop, freedom *not* to write apparently a corrollary of such self-expression. Nonetheless, the volume of mail—often twenty letters a week—in itself makes Vincent feel wanted, and some of the letters truly astonish. (And astonish his siblings, who soon also eagerly await the postman, even the older brother who, always popular with girls, told Vincent that to look for dates through pen-paling would be "like garbage collecting.") It turns out there's a world of people out there—teenagers, housewives in remote places or bad marriages, prison inmates, soldiers—all yearning to connect. "I want to suck your killer cock," writes Ann in Encino, P.O. Box #4. Her first letter. "Eat me with a spoon, then fuck me til I die," writes Heidi in Minneapolis.

After his initial wave of fantasies, Vincent realizes that such letters are not really addressed to him, since of course he's had no chance to present himself to Ann or Heidi, JoAnne or Beatrice, Audrey or Cynthia: these are statements for the page. Autoerotic for the writer. No visible help. Other letters start to arrive, however, which invite an exchange, a revealing of if not the self then the literary self. From teenage girls, talking of their dream lover or date, looking for a shoulder to cry on, to bemoan problems with parents, school, siblings: Life. But here too Vincent is amazed. There's Elise in Chicago, for example, who hates her stepfather, writes that he raped her sister, that she can't sleep at night for fear he'll come through the door, who thinks of herself as fat and ugly though her photo shows otherwise. Who tells Vincent she is so devoted to Adam Ant that in her school yearbook she has been voted "most likely to have Adam Ant's baby."

Taking his cue, in his letters to Elise and others Vincent becomes intellectual guide, psychologist, cheerleader. "Be good to yourself, sweet thing." "If you can't love yourself you can't love anyone else." "Just remember, today is the first day of the rest of your life." "You'll never walk alone." "Take super care of yourself you super fox." Part of the pleasure for Vincent being the transition from reading to writing: though he's always loved books, now he begins to see what it must be like to write one. In his diary, the entries are for himself, to himself; whatever is higher and finer on the page than in life is to justify, motivate, and console only himself. In the letters, however, he's making contact with others, spends hours writing to his best correspondents, and in the process, as if to advance his notion of the distance between this dialogue and the ordinary world, becomes "Vince."

Quite quickly, such virtue is rewarded: pictures start arriving, not just yearbook shots but images less formal, those he reaches out to posing in leather pants and tight tank tops, in provocative or compromising positions. Soon, Rolodex on his desk with one hundred entries, notes on each card to remind him what he's said to whom, a stack of photos in his wallet, Vincent's only problem is the cost of postage. The cost of postage, and the question of the appropriate next step, since as one of his brothers puts it, Vincent has a harem out there. As in, how to get from here to there? Something Vincent ponders until, reading the *Globe* one day, he sees an ad for a Greyhound summer bus pass. Three weeks, unlimited mileage.

Soon Vincent is cleaning bedpans and pushing wheelchairs at a local nursing home Monday and Wednesday afternoons and every other Saturday.

"Doesn't it depress you?" his mother asks.

"What?" Vincent's been curt with his mother for several

years, ever since it dawned on him that she and his father had sexual intercourse to conceive their children. If pushed, Vincent might say that he though he loves his mother he finds such behavior immoral. (More recently, he was disturbed to hear his mother say nude beaches seemed like a good idea, that she wouldn't mind going to one herself. "We're all born naked, aren't we?" she added, laughing, a line which left him irritable for hours.)

"All the old people, sick people, Vincent."

"It's not so bad." A nightmare, actually. Amputees, Alzheimer patients, the lonely. Relatives who visit. Relatives who don't visit. For relief, Vincent decides to up his weekly quota of horror films to two double bills.

Four months later, dog days of August approaching, he's accumulated money for the bus pass and enough stamps to work out his itinerary. To his surprise his parents make no objection to the trip. Can it be, he wonders, that like his siblings they want to see what will happen? And his siblings, well, with a kind of awe and admiration—where did Vincent of all people get the courage?—they stand in Back Bay Terminal with his parents the day his bus pulls out, all of them waving goodbye.

Geek in Evanston—Roberta, actually—had written that she loved Echo and the Bunnymen and Berlin and Tears for Fears and that she wanted to make love with Vincent but would not let him use prophylactics: nothing between them that wasn't organic, she explained. Though Vincent was loath to pass up a sure thing, he'd been turned off when Geek placed an ad in *Fangoria* saying she and Vincent were engaged and then wrote him threatening suicide if he failed to impregnate her. And though he continues to correspond with Elisa in Chicago, early on he got the feeling she had a boyfriend. So forget the Midwest, he decides. Eileen in Reno sounded interesting, but she appeared to be severely overweight in the photo she finally sent, and Mary in Plattsburg had a bad case of acne, grounds for being passed over in the first round, this though Vincent had wrtten her that the soul is the only real source of beauty. Also, enthusiastic about seeing the country, Vincent resolves to begin by going to Los Angeles to visit Janis and then work his way back to Boston.

Following a scenic route of his own devising (which adds an extra seven hundred miles), Vincent spends five days and nights heading west. No showers, no changing his clothes, little sleep, and because the bus shakes so much, to pee into the toilet "requires a sharp eye and steady hand," as he observes in his journal. As for the tap water, the sign says not to drink it, which has the effect of making Vincent reluctant to even wash his hands. Though the bus stops three times a day to give people a chance to grab a meal at some roadside diner, it also picks up or drops off passengers, often in the middle of nowhere, and at refueling everyone has to disembark, no matter what the hour. Worse, because of the route Vincent's chosen, there are layovers, one of the more sobering coming in Las Vegas, which he reaches at 5:00 a.m., the city empty, still, lights going off just before dawn. Nothing glitzy, romantic, exotic, or alluring about it, Vincent thinks, staring at himself in the mirror of the men's room in the station. *"TV deceives,"* he writes in his journal. Cheering himself by rehearsing a joke: "Hear about the cow with short front legs? *Lean* beef."

Imagining the journey before leaving, Vincent had envisioned a wide array of interesting others and the camaraderie of being on the road, but he soon wonders how many different ways you can tell someone about who you are, where you're from, where you're going to. Or hear it from yet another soldier, grandmother, or student. After a while, Vincent tries lying—"My grandmother is very ill"/"My girlfriend is very ill"/ "My best friend is very ill"—but the credulity of others palls. He turns toward the window, adjusts his Walkman, stares out

at the landscape for interminable hours. Writes in his diary that
he is sick of lying, will never lie again. Then adds, *"Hah!!"* As
he reaches the Southwest, swinging through El Paso and Las
Cruces, the bus fills up with Mexican-Americans. Innocent of
any Spanish except "Gracias" and "Adios," Vincent is finally
free to just smile, nod.

Pulling into the LA bus station at eleven at night, he starts
looking for his pen pal Janis. The only problem is that he has
no idea what she looks like, Janis never having sent a photo.
She did confide that her idol is heavy metal star Joan Jett (and
her Blackhearts)—"she's wild and free"—and that her
nickname for herself is Raspy, because of her voice, that she
has brown hair, brown eyes, and is a little over 5 feet tall. For
the next two hours Vincent wanders among the bums, hus-
tlers, runaways, and panhandlers in the station, approaching
any young woman who might remotely qualify—"Janis?
Janis?"—and every few minutes goes to the phone again to try
her number. "She could be almost anybody," Vincent thinks
despairingly, surveying the crowd. At four in the morning
Eastern Standard Time he calls Boston.

"Dad? It's me. Janis didn't show up." Vincent tries not to cry.

"Janis?"

"I'm supposed to stay at her house."

"Tell you what, son. Get a hotel and I'll pay for it later. In
the morning call some of your other pen pals. You have your
Rolodex?"

"Yes. 'Night, Dad. Sorry."

"Don't be sorry, son. Let us know where you end up. We
love you."

Wandering the station for another half hour, finally he hears
a voice behind him. "Vincent?

"Janis?"

"Ja*neece*," she replies in a voice that reminds him of Peter
Lorre. "Ja*neece*."

On the way to her mother's house in the Valley Vincent falls asleep in the car, and, waking briefly after they arrive, takes a shower—the sweetest of his life, he thinks—before crawling between the sheets on the living room couch.

After he wakes at one that afternoon, Janis makes breakfast, asks him perfunctorily about his trip, and then says, matter-of-factly, "I think I just want to be friends."

"Oh," Vincent responds, disappointed but again thinking she sounds like Peter Lorre.

"That means no sex. You don't turn me on. I decided last night. Nothing personal. Everybody has different tastes."

"Oh."

"So, what do you want to do today?"

Trying to make the best of a bad thing, Vincent proposes that they go to Universal Studio. Taking the tour, they see the house used in Hitchcock's *Psycho,* a row of false fronts for westerns, the "Battlestar Galactica" set, the paper-mâché-like shark from *Jaws,* but after a while Vincent realizes this insight into the craft of film isn't making him happy: it all looks tawdry to him, cheap, forlorn. Just too real. Vincent shrugs. If this is understanding how it's done, it suddenly occurs to him, maybe he'd prefer not to know.

That night, Janis and her mother watching TV, he dozes off to the sound of the two of them talking over the soundtrack of a rerun of "The Rockford Files." As always, Jim Garner's in trouble, his attorney—a woman—once more bailing him out. "How long's he going to stay?" Vincent thinks he hears someone ask—Garner/his attorney/Janis/her mother?—before he's completely out.

The next morning, as they sit talking about what to do, Janis says, "Let's go down to the Strip. Sunset Boulevard," she adds, seeing Vincent's puzzled look.

"Sure," he replies, thinking of the stars' names in concrete on the sidewalk.

What Janis has in mind, however, are porno shops and "adult" film houses. "Too early for the hookers," she explains.

After they browse through rows of dildos and magazines in several places and check out the bondage gear, Janis suggests a double bill of *Public Affairs* and *In the Pink.* "My treat," she adds, as though money's the issue. Afraid the cashier will demand ID, Vincent's relieved to get in without trouble, though as he enters the theatre he quickly pretends not to see a sign saying No jacking off in the seats.

Back in the bright light after so many breasts and penises, not having imagined a girl might want to see such films—Janis was the only female in the theatre not on the screen—and not knowing what else to say, Vincent asks Janis if she's ever been there before.

"Why?"

"Just wondered."

"None of your business."

"Sorry." He's silent a moment, then adds: "Did you like it?"

"Stop asking me questions," Janis shouts. "You're making me feel like some kind of freak."

"Not everybody with problems wants to talk about them," Vincent reminds himself, and mutters, "Defense mechanisms," mentally adding the underlining.

The next day Janis drives him to his pen pal Yolanda's house in North Hollywood. "I had several surprises," Vincent writes in his diary that night. "Yolanda's hair is blond now, but it was black in the photo she sent. Also, she has an identical twin sister, Samantha."

The first day, doing errands with the twins and their mother, going to a local park with the three of them for a picnic, unable to tell the sisters apart since Samantha also dyed her hair blond—and both are wearing very tight-fitting *I'm a Chicana* T-shirts—Vincent prudently waits for one or the other to clarify her identity by what she says. A tactic which seems to work, though it leaves him wondering.

The next day he and the twins head off to Venice beach. Thousands of people of all races and colors in the curl of the breaking wave up and down the coast as far as the eye can see. Girls on roller skates flying by on the boardwalk. Perfect bodies, male and female, in every direction. Two quite wonderful bodies on the blanket beside him, each twin wearing a Spandex suit cut to accentuate breasts, hips, buttocks. It had become clear to Vincent that the twins' mother assumed Samantha would act as a chaperone for Yolanda, but as they pass an hour on the blanket and then another, downing hot dogs, French fries, and soft drinks, it dawns on Vincent that the twins not only know what he hopes for but are more than prepared to collaborate with him. Both of them. The key moment being when Samantha—he thinks—picks up an empty Coke can. "Let's play Spin-the-bottle," she says, and soon both girls are kissing Vincent or being kissed by Vincent, each kiss longer, deeper, than the last.

"Vincent's getting excited," Yolanda (??) shouts after several turns of the game. Suddenly enormously pleased with life, instead of yielding to his first impulse—to cover his bathing suit with a towel—Vincent shrugs, sits there beaming.

"Yolanda," Samantha says, "Mother won't be home til late. Let's go."

"Where?" Vincent asks for the sake of making some sound, though he's sure he knows the answer. Already wondering if he'll sleep with both of them and, if so, whether or not it will be both at the same time. If it's only one at a time, Vincent concludes judiciously, it seems only fair he start with Yolanda. And, trudging beside the twins through the sand toward the parking lot, arms full of beach gear, more pleased with life than he can ever remember having been, a joke comes to mind: As the Indian brave said to the mermaid, 'How.' "

The next morning, head throbbing, Vincent records the previous day's events in his diary. "<u>Tragedy</u>," he begins, adding the underlining. Yolanda was driving when they left the beach, the three of them howling with laughter, Vincent happily sandwiched between the twins until . . . until Yolanda rear-ended the car in front of them at a stoplight. At the moment of impact Vincent was thrown forward; his head hit the dash. By the time his head cleared they were back at the house, and when it really cleared again it was time for breakfast, he had a splitting headache, and the twins had been grounded. Worse, their mother was now insisting on taking them with her to visit relatives for a week instead of leaving them at home.

At the bus station the next day, Vincent hugs and kisses Yolanda and Samantha—their mother waiting out in the car—and tells them he'll try to come back when they return. In the meantime, however, he's going east. Though there's Amy in Phoenix and Suzanne in Seattle, Harriet in St. Louis had written "I think I love you, Vincent" some months before, which to an expert if amateur analyst seemed decodeable as "I want to make love to you."

Later that day, bus rolling east through the desert, Vincent tries to imagine Harriet's house, being met by Harriet at the station, how they'll end up making love. He's certain it will happen, though he can't really picture the moment either as an extension of what he was doing with the twins or as a variant of what he saw in the porno theatre. Too many unknowns, though even so he's certain it will happen. But then his mind skips forward to the day after they make love: Harriet's angry with him and stays angry the rest of the time he's there, her mother and father nonetheless extremely—strangely—supportive, as if in favor of what he's doing with their daughter.

Shrugging, reminding himself of the power of positive thinking, looking out the window at the mountains in the distance, Vincent begins to imagine coming home when the trip is done. Arriving in Boston, but, since the family is up in New Hampshire for Labor Day, making a final ride on his Greyhound pass, out to Springfield, then taking a Vermont Transit bus for which he has to pay with his last five dollar bill.

Which brings him via Brattleboro to Keene and thus to the moment of walking up the long gravel driveway of his family's summer house with two dollars and change in his pocket, pack and Rolodex on his back.

Bus rolling eastward, next scheduled stop Gallup, New Mexico, Tucumcari and Amarillo soon to follow, surrounded by seated Latinos and Indians clustered in threes, temporarily giving up trying to get a better look at the girl sitting alone in the row in front of him—should he start a conversation with her?—Vincent tastes the moment once again, with tears coming to his eyes pictures himself starting up the long gravel driveway of the summer house, siblings there as he comes into view, all of them suddenly waving, clapping, cheering, shouting "Vincent's back, he's here, it's Vincent," elated that he's really home after such an unbelievable voyage, after such awesomely incredible adventures, after so many, many miles.

* * *

'A Land of Men & Women too'

WHAT A WORLD, SHE thinks, reading the morning *Chron,* both girls already off to preschool. Random shootings on freeways, condoms for prisoners, free needles for junkies. Trapped in forty-mile-long fishing nets, whales are not only dying but perceived to be competing with humans for scarce resources. We have no visitors from outer space because as a culture achieves space travel it simultaneously overruns the capacity to control its technology. I'm taking in too much data, she thinks, doing the dishes. The homeless, Tiananmen Square, cold fusion, the ozone layer, and, for a moment, peace breaking out: Gorby, the Berlin wall. We don't build elaborate tombs for our dead in California, a priest is quoted as saying, because cemeteries are really for the living: a transient people, we'll soon be moving elsewhere. My soul/ my suburb, she thinks, putting in a wash after going out for diapers. Sitting down to check out the Yankees box score in the Sporting Green, still following the daily fate of a team her father grew up watching in a city three thousand miles away. Scanning the stats for the hint of another Mantle, Ford, DiMaggio. Is Don Mattingly, for instance, an Immortal?

Though most weekday nights the four years they were

married, running the household with first the one baby daughter and then the second, she cooked her husband dinner from yet another recipe out of Sunset Magazine, when the good life palled he broke her jaw. She'd had an affair to compensate for his increasingly staccato gruffness, rudeness, belligerence, testiness, ever more monosyllabic lack of grace. *Staccato*—his normal cadence, a kind of verbal karate chop, only adding insult to injury, though she savored the onomatopoeia when the word first conjured itself up in her mind to describe how he spoke. This at a time she was taking ballet twice a week not just to get in shape, sweating in leotard and tights, but for the *adagio* of dance, the *duende*. She'd had an affair, in any case, nothing to really write home about, as she told her girlfriend next door, though sex and sinsemilla in the hot tub at his place in Muir Beach, on the cliff with a view down the coast the ten miles to San Francisco, was picturesque, and then she told her husband she'd had the affair, not exactly to get even but to let him know there was some kind of equal something at work in the world, at which point, girls upstairs sleeping, he broke her jaw with one punch. And then stormed out of the house and, soon after, sued for divorce. Did all the paperwork himself, the cheapskate, though of course for propriety's sake—and attorneys always had to be proper, he'd conveyed so many times—he filtered it through the office mail under his partner's signature.

Which brings up the first thing she had to learn about men: never, ever marry an attorney, because if and when you divorce (as you may well, despite or because of TV/nouvelle cuisine/cappuccinos/postmodernism), your former spouse will kill you in the property settlement. Which brings up the second thing she had to learn about men: never, ever marry an attorney and have children with him in this dolphin-loving/rain-forest-saving nation of recyclers. Particularly not girl children, because if and when you divorce, your former spouse will kill you forever and ever, not only turning the children against you, suggesting explicitly and implicitly every second weekend when he has custody (except for when he doesn't want to see his daughters whom he loves more than any father could because he has to go to Tahoe to ski or has important business—*everything* being business, actually, that fraud invented by men for men), intimating that they, his daughters, can love and please Daddy as Mommy never had the legs/hips/lips to. Nor, she learned, should you let an attorney father your children because then, every inch of the way, on issues of child support/shared medical bills/custody time/fees for swim class, etc., etc., then all that accredited legal training and member-of-the-bar dues-paid and socially condoned killer instinct will be brought to bear on … *you*. "Mammas, don't let your babies grow up to be cowboys," she heard Willie Nelson sing. Oh, it made her laugh and then made her cry: Mammas, don't let your little girls grow up to marry attorneys.

Attorneys: she got murdered by hers in the divorce, a woman, framed sheepskins on the wall, suit like a man's, incompetent or coopted by the opposition she could never quite tell. But at least finally she had the divorce. Called herself a widow, for the laugh—would that it were true—but of course now she was a divorcee at twenty-six, damn it, a kind of failure, single parent with a bad alimony and support settlement, and even if they'd stayed married the fucker would never have predeceased her. She thought of remarrying, but then decided there had to be something more, so she went back to school part-time. Finishing her B.A. would lead her toward a job eventually, she figured, a teaching credential or something on that order. But, she noticed, nothing in the least bit contemporary in the catalog much interested her: no deconstruction, no women's studies, no ethnic studies, no psychology. She was after what had survived. Fell in love with Blake, Rembrandt, with the words Apollonian and Dionysian, with the sounds

Daphnis, Chloe, and Persephone, spoke of one of her pro-
fessors as "my mentor."

Also, despite her bias against self-help books and/or the
notion that we are all victims, nonetheless, reading a magazine article on BART one day, she decided she had low self-
esteem. Of course she did: her father wanted a boy, had told
her so, and her mother had always been cold as ice. Not
antagonistic, just not warm. She'd once thought it was because parents loved her sister more. Her sister, six years older,
understandably unhappy once a sibling arrived. But then,
when her sister killed herself in a car crash at nineteen, into
drugs and a bad love affair, she thought her parents somehow
blamed it on her. Another eight years later, however, when her
father died her senior year in college, looking down at him in
the coffin and accepting that he never wanted her, she said to
herself, "Goodbye, Daddy, you asshole." Thought of the dead
Yankee greats. Wept. And then accepted her boyfriend's offer
of marriage, impelled by fact that she was already two months
pregnant. Time as a widow passed. She framed her daughters'
finger paintings. Picked nasturtiums in her garden. Heard the
phrase "Kyrie eleison" as if never before, though in choir in
high school she'd often sung the words. "Lord have mercy,"
she muttered, putting away leftovers, not about to start going
to church again. Stood in the mirror examining her breasts,
wondering who should hold them. Saw the paint peeling in
the living room, behind the rabbit cage. Her mentor, the
classics professor, tumbled out of the crown of a huge red-
wood—she never did understand what he'd been doing up
there, but gathered it had something to do with Art—and then,
still wearing a cast on his arm, he tried to get her to sleep with
him, wouldn't see her in office hours after being rebuffed. But
still she continued to feel exalted by what she was reading.
Kafka, Virginia Woolf, Confucius, Rilke, Beckett. There were
secrets out there, something truer, The Truth. Felt she was

getting closer when she produced a term paper on baseball and hubris.

She met a guy she liked at a dinner party, liked him from the start because he ignored her date completely, talked to her as if they had every right to talk because theirs was a true meeting of the minds. So they left the party together, drove to her girlfriend's. Just in time, because there was a potluck in progress for Sensual Suburbia, a kind of Tupperware party scheme for neighbors to merchandise sexual paraphernalia to neighbors, with the result that before they ever went to bed they were examining "Anal intruders," "Ben Wa balls," cock rings, vibrators, body oils, and "edible undies" for both men and women. Passing up "Nympho Cream" and "Joy Jell," settling for incense and a tube of KY jelly, they headed over to her place, where she told him the story of her divorce: "I'm a widow; my husband beat me," she began, and then did a hula for him. A real hula, since she'd taken classes as a girl. After which she explained how Kyrie eleison would come to mind, how she felt like Odysseus, like Sylvia Plath, like Frida Kahlo, like Thurman Munson.

Later, when they were in bed, she told him, "Pretend you're saying you love me."

"Pretend I just was," he responded, and they both laughed.

She licked the small of his back, sucked the toes of his right foot, thought of a line from the fragments of the Greek poet Archilochus: "the seam of/the scrotum."

"Who's Thurman Munson?" he finally asked, which greatly increased her respect for him.

Somewhat later, just as he began to enter her, she'd been about to say, "Can you believe my life?"

* * *

Citizen Mad Dog

*T*HREE YEARS OF PRISON in his early twenties for motor vehicle theft, known as Mad Dog: too violent when provoked to bother with. Thriving despite being one of the small minority of whites inside. Bad break, to be busted in the South. Promoted to running the laundry long before he got a release date, impeccable in his upgraded prison issue, resplendent in starched shirt and tailored pants. The unspoken logic of so hostile an environment something like: Care for yourself and so be worthy of being cared for by others, were they only here to care for you, though of course they're not.

Finally out on parole, Mad Dog immediately disappeared, basketball in his pack, wandering the country shooting hoops in college towns, always reading another book—especially the latest Updike, when the setting was coastal Massachusetts—until after three years and thirty-five states the clock on his sentence expired and, turning twenty-seven, he was a free man.

Returning to Boston, he went right up to the North Shore, to Ipswich, bars full of the Poles and Greeks he came of age drinking with. Bannon's at Depot Square, then the Choate Bridge Pub ("Oldest stone arch bridge on the North American

41

continent," people would say when he was a kid). Waiting around town most of the day until his father finally walked by.

"Hey, what do you know? Shit floats to the surface. My own lost son Richard."

"Nice to see you too, Dad."

"So what do you want?"

"Nothin'. Really. I come back to give you somethin'."

"You can try." Mad Dog's father was forty-eight, five nine/ two fifty, a hod carrier. Strong as a bastard, to use the local vernacular. Never known to back away from a fight, graced with an amazingly high tolerance for physical pain. And, in a way, prudent: armed. For a long time he carried a gun, once pulled it when Mad Dog tried to settle things between them.

"No firearms today, Dad?" Mad Dog said, studying him carefully. "Tough luck. Anyway, I got a short speech prepared. Which is: you fucked over me and Danny and David and Ellen with all that brutal shit. I could let it go, smoke some dope, say, 'That's just the way it was,' but you wouldn't, would you, Dad? Or I could say, 'The poor alkie stumblebum couldn't help himself, if he had just gotten better medical help ...' Blah, blah, blah ... But that's fuckin' liberal bullshit meaning take it in the ass again. Right, Dad?"

"You been takin' it in the ass, jailbird? Convict cocksucker."

Mad Dog nodded: his father was helping. Just to see his father after so long clarified things, not to mention being reminded of his father's special way with words. So Mad Dog feinted with a left jab and shot out a short kick to the right knee, hearing it crack, and as his father went down Mad Dog kicked him in the stomach, then real quick grabbed his hair, slamming his head against the pavement. His father lying there groaning, spitting blood, the barfly unemployed Greeks and Poles watching as Mad Dog pulled down his zipper and pissed on his old man.

"Farewell, Updike Country," Mad Dog shouted as he walked away. He'd had a job mowing the writer's lawn one summer years before, felt a connection. Humming "California Here I Come," he went down South Main Street past the old Town Hall to Argilla Road. He just really needed one last look at Crane's Beach before heading west, before the Ipswich police could catch up with him.

There are people who have a bad childhood and want to get started on children of their own as soon as possible. And then there are people who have a bad childhood and want never to bring a child of their own into this vale of tears. Mad Dog, despite having raised and loved his younger siblings, protecting them when his parents were "blind, stinkin' drunk," being of the latter persuasion. And that would have been it, except for his non-wife Rita. Who, after nearly ten years with Richard, decided she wanted kids. Insisted she wanted them right now, since she was turning thirty. That if not, she'd leave him. All of which he failed to take seriously until Rita had the locks changed and got a restraining order from the court to keep him away. From his own fuckin' apartment! Pissing him off mightily, but in the end he went with Rita to see a therapist—a lesbian, he was certain—and had to sit there and promise not to hit Rita ever again and not to drink so much and to be more sensitive to her needs and to try to get her pregnant.

"Hey, one question," Mad Dog interjected. "Do I have to sleep with her?" Adding, "Just kidding," when the therapist scowled. "Joke. Joke." Holding up his hands as if the therapist had him covered.

So he and Rita did sleep together, for the first time in months, since Richard was usually dead drunk when she came home from work, but though it was just once, once was enough.

"Our love is not to be denied," Mad Dog said some months later, contemplating Rita's swollen belly. Knocking back another beer for medicinal purposes.

Rita. Richard had argued that he actually was a Bhudda in

dealing with her, even if he did occasionally get rough, since she was bedeviled by both premenstrual syndrome and post-menstrual syndrome: headaches, short temper, disorientation, peevishness. "What it comes down to," Richard told the therapist, "is you have maybe five days a month when she's herself, or, put another way, when she's a fuckin' human being. You want to know who's the victim here, *I'm* the victim. Plus," he added, "she's redneck white trash. You're still stuck with some Eleanor Roosevelt bullshit you learned in social work school: everyone the same, Family of Man. Well let me tell you. What bein' redneck white trash in America means is that her whole family is vicious, alcoholic, and stupid. That her parents came from parents who were vicious, alcoholic, and stupid. It means she can't help bein' vicious and stupid herself a lot of the time even if she's dead cold sober, pushin' me, tryin' to make me mad. Takin' a swing at me. You have any idea how many times I haven't hit back? Such as, ninety-nine point nine percent of the time?"

Mad Dog stared at the therapist. "Really, lady, these ideas of yours, they're how things *should* be, maybe. Well here's a should: you should try walkin' a mile in my shoes sometime. I just look like a fuckin' monster."

Hair cropped, jowls enormous, no neck in sight. Not really a monster, though you will concede that the bloom of Mad Dog's youth does seem to have departed. He was 5'9"/170 when he took on his old man that day in Ipswich. Now, thirteen years later, turning forty, he's fifty pounds heavier. His father's size. "The fruit always falls close to the foot of the tree," Mad Dog opines, putting down another beer, one of his ten a day. Eight to ten being what it takes to maintain. This in conjunction with the prescription anti-depressants.

And if the social worker ever takes up Richard's challenge to walk a mile in his shoes, it will have to be with arch supports—all those years of jump shots on asphalt playgrounds. Yet even then the question will arise, Which shoes, since at any given moment Richard owns perhaps thirty pairs of sneakers. Three new pairs of The Pump: the Imelda Marcos of basketball footwear.

Mad Dog as househusband, taking care of his son—Danny, named after his brother—five and a half days a week. Rita working at the restaurant four days a week, getting one and a half days off, then taking over with the kid. Richard endlessly patient during what he calls "my shift," wanting to be there for his son. No day care, no babysitters: he'll take care of it. Putting another wash into the machine. Mopping the floor. Doing the dishes. Taking out the trash. Bringing Danny with him everywhere, all day. Tucking him under his arm like a loaf of bread when Danny's small. Determined to stay put for at least five years to give him the security and continuity Richard deems essential to trust. What Richard himself never received. Giving Danny as much freedom as possible, trying to keep the boundaries simple and clear. And for Rita one rule only: nobody hits the kid, no matter what he does. Send him to his room, fine, tap him on the butt, but that's it. Period.

Ipswich. Crane's Beach, miles of shore and dune running up from the river. Fried clams in summer, fresh corn on the cob, blueberries. Taking the train into Fenway or hitching in to see the Sox. The town's colonial homes, Mad Dog growing up in a house that was run down but built before 1800. Liking the idea so many people had lived there before. Shooting hoops over at Linebrook playground in summer, inside the Episcopal church gym when it started to get cold. Pellucid autumn days, the intensity of the turning leaves often making him nod in appreciation, as if watching virtuosi, sobered only by the threat of the coming interminable winter. Depressing perhaps because of the relative absence of light, or because it was the season his father would really get mean.

Just one time was Richard surprised when his father hit him. That is, usually Richard could figure out the sequence in his father's mind. Not that it was fair or right, but it could be divined. Once, however, right after they left his grandmother's, as they got in the car his father wacked him behind the head very hard, knocking him into the dash, breaking his nose. Richard must have been nine. It took him a while, but finally it came clear. Of course: his grandmother had showed him affection.

Mad Dog's economics. The rent-controlled apartment is 200/month plus utilities, two bedroom with a view of the hills. 550/month tax free from Social Security for having convinced them he's crazy—which on the other hand he is—plus free medical and dental plus food stamps. Then Rita earns maybe 20 K working as a waitress four days a week. And after that there are the credit cards. Sit still long enough, they start coming in: Richard has five in his name, five in Rita's. Then occasional constuction work under the table—another five K per annum, maybe—and the gambling. Despite some heavy losses at blackjack up at Reno, Richard does know sports. In 1988, for instance, during spring training, he took the Dodgers to win the Series. A 25-1 shot, but at season's end there was gimpy-legged Kirk Gibson hitting that home run off Dennis Eckersley and young Orel Hershiser having the week of his life. Mad Dog, looking like a genius, immediately buying two reclining chairs for the living room, new washer-dryer, and video cam to film the kid. All quality stuff.

Add to this the occasional shoplifting of expensive records, then returning them to the store for a credit slip to sell at a discount for cash, or the weekly prime beef lifted from the Yuppie market down on Telegraph, and the stolen gear available on a regular basis over at People's Park, and you have . . . well, something resembling a lower-middle class standard of living. "Figure the equivalent of forty-five K per annum," Mad

Dog says, doing his books. "Maybe thirty-two K tax-free."

California. Mad Dog hates it. Perhaps because having found some place he can survive, he's constantly reminded he'd have been dead if he'd stayed in Ipswich like his brother Danny. Or his sister Ellen, a drug addict who might as well be dead. David having gotten out too, living in a van somewhere up in Oregon, a small-time burn artist. So while California has given Richard shelter, it's exile. A place he's not from, where people just don't understand where he's coming from, what might have shaped him. Why he's there at all. Which is to say, what's true. "Phoney, stupid, know-nothing, no-class mother-fuckers," Mad Dog often says, speaking of Californians. "Superficial. Bigoted. Slime. Shallow scumbags."

Mad Dog on his day off from Danny, over at the Bear's Lair on the Cal campus knocking back a few beers, one of the football players aching to push him around. Mad Dog simply giving the would-be stud a two-handed shove on the chest, hard, sending him across to the wall, leaving it at that. But why not teach the dumb fuck something more? Why? Because Mad Dog can't risk being sent away from Danny. Shit: ex-con non-student? Assault with intent? C'mon, they'd throw away the key. "Cramps my academic freedom, havin' a kid," he says thoughtfully as he sips his beer, looking over at the football player, thinking what else he could teach him.

Mad Dog as instructor, a role he savors. Working with Danny on each new skill, always patient. Or trying to show some teenager on the court how to improve his jump shot, willing to stay there for hours if need be. Or Mad Dog in a bar, telling the man on the next stool—"I ain't shittin' you, buddy"—that he just doesn't know what he's talking about. About the prospects for a given year's phenom hitting fifty home runs, for example. "But he's already got thirty-one and we're not even at the All-Star break," the man says. "So put your money where your mouth is," Mad Dog replies, as usual not unwilling to inform. "Give me two to one on a hundred?" Mad Dog also gets into it with one of the local cops. The problem starts one night when the man pulls him over for rolling through a stop sign, then cuffs him with his hands behind his back, concluding by roughing Mad Dog up for mouthing off about being cuffed with his hands behind his back. "Fuckin' dwarf," Mad Dog shouts when the cop tells him to put his hands behind his back. "Fuckin' Puerto Rican dwarf," though he knows the man is Chinese. The cop responding by punching him in the stomach, then kicking him in the small of the back.

By the time a second officer arrives, Mad Dog is more than ready to explain where it all went wrong. "See," he says to the black lieutenant, a former Cal linebacker who's something like six five, "this little prick has a complex. Too short. You know I'm no trouble to any cop who plays by the rules. But this mini-dirtbag's on a trip. Maybe this is the only way he can get it up. You oughta buy him elevator shoes."

"Cut him loose," the lieutenant tells the cop who cuffed Mad Dog, trying not to smile. "Cut the crazy bastard loose."

Which would have been it, except that on his days off from Danny Mad Dog follows the Chinese cop around town with his video cam, just waiting to document his next mistake. "Bill of Rights," he often shouts at the cop. "Bill of fuckin' Rights, little cocksucker."

Mad Dog's mother. Though she was also a drunk, though she frequently beat him when he was young, he settled things with her early on, cracking her jaw when he turned thirteen, one quick punch that completely changed the balance of power between them. More, whatever made her tick was so alien to him that he regarded her as another species, beyond understanding, to be judged only by her behavior. She was a lush, she was bitter that Mad Dog's father had abandoned her for a younger woman she always called "The Thing," she was utterly selfish and seemed to have no instinct to love or to protect her children. That's all Mad Dog could figure out, and, really, all it seemed necessary to know.

Nonetheless, having been out of touch with his mother for years, as Danny turns two Mad Dog has the impulse to try to salvage something for him. Some predecessors to identify with, lineage, history, continuity. Something more than the Cal ring Mad Dog wears, class of '72. Authentic, but of course not his. Who wouldn't want this for his child? Nonetheless, when Rita asks if he's thinking of inviting his mother to come out to California, he replies: "Are you crazy? How could we ever trust her around Danny? We couldn't."

"But don't *you* want to see her, Richard?"

"You know, Rita, my mother could eat shit and die as far as I'm concerned. No offense, but as far as that goes I have no regrets your father died last year and that your mother's too weak to get on a plane. No disrespect, but she has the mind of a five-year-old."

"Don't talk about my parents that way," Rita shouts.

"Right," Mad Dog responds. "Right. I know what you mean. The truth really hurts."

Mad Dog and insomnia. Since he was a child, he's frequently been unable to sleep through the night. Maybe it began with waiting for his father to come home, to see if his father would be looking for someone to knock around. Whatever the reason, frequently Richard's up late, TV on, sitting there alone, and often he thinks of The National on 4th Street in St. Petersburg. A place he discovered years before while running out his parole. A drunk box, dollar a shot, nice and dark in back, easy on a drinker's tender eyes, several pinball machines, pyramid of hard booze bottles behind the bar. "When I'm upset about my lot," Mad Dog says, "when I truly despair of my condition, when I think it wasn't fair what happened to

me or my brothers and sister, when I get my father on the
brain, I try to make myself change the station in my mind, so
to speak. And then I think of The National in St. Pete's." He
laughs. "You know," he adds, "if I ever disappear, if I just can't
take it anymore, give me a week or two, then look for me
down at The National. Most days I'll be comin' in around
noon."

* * *

Zenobia In New York

*L*ATE MAY IN MANHATTAN, overcast, very humid, and very hot, the threat of rain. Walking through Central Park beyond the Metropolitan toward the reservoir by the Guggenheim, sky ever darker, Zenobia—Zeno, for short—thinks, "Time to find shelter" as she sees two Rhodesian ridgebacks go by, says to herself, "They belong on the veranda of some farm in the veldt." Right after which several horsemen pass, putting Zeno in mind of how she almost got a job driving a carriage around the park. That is, Zeno met a woman in a diner over on 9th Avenue who was a driver and offered to introduce her to the owner of the stable. Something Zeno gave thought to before deciding against it by not deciding, balked primarily by the image of horses laboring on asphalt in the summer heat.

Nearby, several kids torment a squirrel, but Zeno's attention is diverted by a passing golden retriever. Just then a jogger steams past with an aging German shepherd on leash trailing miserably behind. "That's simply not right," Zeno says out loud, as if to an assembly of fairminded observers, and adds, "Shepherds are very loyal." Staring for a moment at the bend around which dog and man have disappeared, thinking this

51

mistreatment of a noble animal must be stopped, she takes off after them just as the downpour begins, flashes of lightning and several claps of thunder for a moment stilling the sirens, horns, and undifferentiated roar of the city.

Later, soaked, passing the Senegalese street vendors selling fake Rolexes, after stepping in to the Greek joint on the corner near her apartment for some souvlaki, Zeno takes the subway downtown, holds on to a strap and sways as the train accelerates, as a bare-chested black man in dreadlocks, torn shorts, and bare feet comes through the rear door of the car carrying a paper cup. "I need some money. I don't want to rob, but I am hungry. I don't want to hurt nobody. Just give me some money." Teenage black girls snickering, as if his pitch just doesn't cut it.

Living room of an apartment on the Upper West Side, Zeno maid of honor at the wedding of her friend Flo. Flo's third marriage, this time to an investment counselor who's had trouble with alcohol and drugs. On their first date, resolved to seduce him, Flo left the front door ajar, placed herself in the bath. "Come on in" she shouted, as she heard the doorbell. Reaching the doorway of the bathroom, her husband-to-be fainted: when he was three, Flo later learned, his mother died of a heart attack while bathing him.

Now, Flo stands with him under the huppa, hip rabbi performing the ceremony before the thirty guests. "Kiss the bride," the rabbi says, but, when Flo and her husband embrace, adds, "I told you to kiss, not consummate." After the ceremony, quite sure the rabbi's used the line before, Zeno confronts him, says, "That was cheap, very cheap. Shame on you."

Later, Flo's mother-the-psychic, adding hors d'oeuvres to her enormous girth, observes, "Perhaps now my daughter Flo's finally learned to find peace in herself." Then, wiping her mouth with a napkin, she graps Zeno's right hand, inspects the palm. "This is serious," she says. "Come see me soon."

"You must get outside yourself," Flo's mother tells Zeno the following week. "Your biggest trouble is, what do you really want? You've already lived more than a quarter of a century. You're ravenous but you forget to eat. You sought your freedom, and now you have it. *Use it.*" And, pausing: "What did you say your sign is?"

One of Zeno's many returns to Manhattan. The jet's long slow glide up the west side of the island above the Hudson, then a languid right turn toward LaGuardia above Columbia University. Sunset, the buildings like dominos, World Trade Center/ Chrysler Building/Empire State Building. Zeno—so close to the ground now, appproaching human scale—no longer afraid of being airborne.

Back in New York. "Sometimes I'm frightened," Zeno tells her mother on the phone, "I get on the subway and want to bolt like a horse. Why me, here? What journey am I on?"

"Don't be theatrical," her mother says, theatrically.

Good thing I'm not in need of protection, Zeno thinks.

"And try to dress up more," her mother adds. "I really wish you'd work on it."

"If I can't have boys, then for the love of God give me a warrior queen," Zeno's father always said. Septima Zenobia, ruler of Palmyra, who conquered several of Rome's eastern provinces before being subjugated. According to the '39 Encyclopaedia Britannica, family reference work during Zeno's childhood, Zenobia was a "remarkable woman, famed for her beauty, her masculine energy and unusual powers of mind ..." who "exceeded her husband in talent and ambition." And, "The queen refused to yield to Aurelian's demand for surrender and drew up her army at Emesa for the battle which was to decide her fate. In the end she was defeated, and there was nothing for it but to fall back upon Palmyra across the desert.

Thither Aurelian followed her in spite of the difficulties of transport, and laid siege to the well-fortified and provisioned city. At the critical moment the queen's courage seems to have failed her; she and her son fled the city to seek help from the Persian king, they were captured on the bank of the Euphrates, and the Palmyrenes, losing heart at this disaster, capitulated ..."

Zeno grew up with this version of her namesake, and though inspired by the tone, of course she had questions, continues to wonder. *"Her courage seems to have failed her ..."* In the 1979 Brittanica's version, for example, which Zeno peruses at the Public Library at 42nd Street, Zenobia instigated the assasination of her husband and stepson, then "styled herself queen."

"Zenobia's career made a deep impression on the Roman writers of the collection of biographies known as the *Historia Augusta* ("August History," probably 4th century). They compared her to the Egyptian queen Cleopatra (1st century B.C.) and recounted—not always reliably—stories regarding her dark beauty, chastity, learning, and fabulous wealth. She is known to have studied Greek literature with the philospher Cassius Longinus. According to some sources, she saved her life at the time of her capture by blaming Longinus and her other advisers for Palmyra's aggression, and they were subsequently executed."

"Revisionist!" Zeno says out loud, stalking out of the library.

New York City, 1986. *Littering is dirty and selfish and don't do it.* A street sign a la Mayor Koch. New York as Calcutta. Primal soup. The homeless and other euphemisms. Investment bankers all the rage. The realm of the fiscal being extended, Zeno observes, transactions not previously seen as monetary now part of the cash economy. Used cardboard fruit cartons being sold at the Korean fruit markets, for example. Potential mates calibrating each other's net worth. A city of certainties. Everyone knows what's what, what they want: *more, out.* Zeno long since familiar with the nuances of finance, daughter of parents raised in wealth who managed to disinherit themselves of everything but their social status, the "wherewithal" to maintain that status perennially a concern, if unmentionable.

Zeno's New York. Biking home through the park from fabric design work on her used white Raleigh three-speed against a steady stream of joggers, skaters, and cyclists, past Cleopatra's needle and the model boat basin. Papers and empty beer cans flying up llth Ave, icebergs floating out to sea on the Hudson. Ballet class. Yoga class. Capoeira class. Christmas Eve at the cathedral of St. John the Divine. Chestnut and pretzel vendors loading up their carts on 9th Ave. Down to the foodstalls under the overpass for Yugolsav goat cheese, Amish chickens, celery root and apples, sake and Italian bread. Ailanthus tree budding in the courtyard, gutters swimming. Parrots in the oaks, blown up on a hurricane.

Zeno's fifth floor apartment in Hell's Kitchen. Rent controlled. One seventy-two/month. View of the river. Ten units, no elevator. A steal. Her building part of a blue-collar New York fast disappearing, developers fighting for it, neighborhood going upscale fast. Soon to hold no more workers, dancers, actors, musicians.

Her apartment: living room, bedroom, small kitchen, tub across from the stove, tiny bathroom. Air shaft, diesel fumes, noise of many households. (Zeno rescuing a pigeon trapped in the air shaft by someone who nailed a screen over the opening.) Pile of lumber for the bookcases she's building. Self-designed cotton sleeping bag. Pair of light green corduroy pants in progress. Swaths of quilt material under the sleeping William-the-cat. (Abandoned in the subway; saved by Zenobia.)

E. B. White's *Charlotte's Web* on the floor beside her, Zeno reads Vicki Hearne on language, interspecies communication,

and *virtu*, Hearne arguing that "a story about how what appears to be horse insanity may be ... evidence of how powerful equine genius is, and how powerfully it can object to incoherence ... The stories we tell matter ..."
Zeno, reading this, feeling elevated, confirmed.

Zeno on her childhood. "Once we were down by the boathouse and a bobcat came up. A bobcat! That's a kind of lynx, a wildcat. It had tufted ears, it was the size of a dog, something like an border collie. It was just standing there, looking hungry, so I fed him my sandwich. Then I went back to the house for more food and turned to find him trailing behind me. A bobcat! There was also a pair of ravens that sat on a railing. I'd put my eyes to my hands when they passed. Of course there were raccoons, possum, rabbits, garter snakes, orange newts, toads, box turtles, what-have-you.

"There were always fireflies. Sometimes you'd see one caught in the spider's web in the back room.

"There'd be sun in the meadow beyond under the trees, day-lilies and butterfly weed in bloom, fresh-cut cherry wood stacked by the shed, hornbeam and wild swamp azalea. Moss. Lichen (a word I've always loved)."

And once, at her family's summer place, Zeno lay spread-eagled in the pasture surrounded by the neighbor's five cows. Their white faces lowered over her, she says years later, remembering, "the heat of their exhalations very moist, gossamer wisps of saliva falling. Tears in their eyes." Later, the five of them sat circled around her, "shoulders and spines visible above the waves of grass like the humps of five russet whales."

Zeno at nine, yearning. High up on the four-poster in the lavender bedroom that faces out to sea, Venetian blinds softly rattling in the off-shore breeze, long lavender curtains stirring fitfully. Zeno sprawled on a white cotton sheet, drinking goat's milk from a monogrammed glass. Thinking of how, that morning, an enormous blue heron stared as she pretended to be very busy collecting sand dollars.

A childhood dream. Great white osprey soaring with Zeno on its shoulders, small feathers cascading down with each pulse of wings. Zeno putting the feathers in her jewelbox, "to show—like milk teeth, or Grandmother's Mesopotamian spun-gold earrings that ring like bells—to strangers."

Zeno tells these stories to Jacques, a Haitian from her capoeira class, whose heavily-accented English is less than fluent. At her invitation he spends the night on a mat in the living room instead of going all the way back uptown to his place, but not as her lover. Or, not yet; Zeno's thinking it through. She likes Jacques in part because he excels at copoeira, in which the Portuguese verb for fighting is *jogar*, to play. Zeno also has the feeling that Jacques understands play in the sense that animals understand it: frisking, butting, just pronging along on all fours, skidaddling; the sheer sport of being alive. But in her mind she also pictures going to Jacques' home in Haiti with him, falling off the map of the known world, being lost to all she's lived thus far, like the great European women explorers of the nineteenth century. And this she has to think through.

Play. Animals. Often Zeno sees people as animals, wishes them more like animals or that they'd admit the resemblance. Humans, Zeno thinks, reluctant to acknowledge any essential connection to behavior routinely manifested in the 'lower' world: cannibalism, infanticide, fratricide, parricide, the impulse to dominate. And as for sex, people seem determined to diminish the power of what's involved, the insanely volatile mix of fear and attraction, the threat of mutual aggression. What Zeno loves in the animal kingdom are the rituals of courtship, the chases—dances!—of cheetahs, for example, female with harem of males in pursuit before she exhausts all but the one with whom she'll copulate. Play-fighting, play-biting, pouncing: courtship to moderate tensions of conflict-

ing desires. Females at the penultimate moment raising one
leg as if to ward off danger; males and females sinking their
teeth into each other's necks, drawing blood. Or the male
spider working hard to convey to his potential lover that he's a
mate, not dinner. Or screams modified into songs: the complex morning duets—calls and whoops—of gibbon pairs, audible for miles across southeast Asian forests as they an-
nounce the dawn.

Zenobia as her own doctor, practicing without a license,working not just for health but for regeneration. A diet
of live fresh foods and sprouting seeds. Garden essences for
balancing, cleansing: celery, to restore the immune system;
cucumber, for reattaching to life during depression; dill, to
assist in reclaiming power one has released to others; okra, for
returning the ability to see the positive; and comfrey, to repair
soul damage in a past or present lifetime.

Sure, it sounds ludicrous, Zeno acknowledges, measured
by the standards of western science. But what, she asks, what
has that science produced now? Beside the threat of nuclear
war/chemical poisons in our food/endless torture of animals?

And to whom does Zeno say this? To her father, of course,
university researcher, expert on light coherent and incoherent,
romantic whose song is the song of science. Her mother
chiming in, "Oh, Zeno, do leave the poor man alone." Zeno
then announcing plans to be in Central Park for the Harmonic
Convergence, the organizers' intent to have at least 144,000
humans get together around the world to hold hands and
chant—"to resonate in harmony." The plan to help Earth
synchronize itself with the rest of the galaxy. Thus to prevent
extinction of many species, including humans.

"Oh," her mother says. "Must you?" Zeno thinking of the
various phyla in which mothers are known to sacrifice their
children. Remembering being in the back of the Volvo station
wagon yet once again as a child, being taken somewhere,

somewhere, by her mother. Realizing how much she resembles her mother. Her father pouring himself another shot of Glenfiddich, asking, "Have you bought health insurance yet? You must have health insurance."

"Yes, Daddy, " Zeno replies, thinking of the mice, monkeys, and cats on which his lab performs research. The word abattoir coming to mind.

"You don't want to end up an eccentric spinster, do you?" her mother adds. "Well, do you?"

"I'm struggling with what I want to commit to and what is possible," Zeno tells Flo, whose marriage to the investment counselor is already in trouble. Zeno thinking it might be easiest—having been up at the Cloisters earlier, looking at the medieval tapestries—if someone simply gave her a castle for which she could be chatelaine. Where she could wait for her unicorn.

Zeno deciding she's not ready for Jacques, the Haitian. That Harry, the film editor who's been wooing her with travel and jazz, just doesn't have any idea who she really is, doesn't want to know, that a match with him would be "wildly inappropriate." That he can't see beyond her blond hair. ("What's the matter with liking blond hair?" Flo shouts.) That having two sexes for reproduction in mammals may simply have been an evolutionary wrong turn. "Parthenogensis," Zeno says to Flo. "Hermaphrodites!" Suddenly thinking of a quilt with a flying goose pattern, or perhaps something with giraffes.

"Well, I want a *man* in my bed, thank you," Flo says, "not just some cat." Zeno not reminding Flo that at least feline testosterone level seems immune to fluctuations in the stock market.

Zeno up late, pulling out her Halliburton's *Book of Marvels*. "In affairs of state [Zenobia] astonished the ministers with her wisdom. In the army the generals marveled at her bravery . . .

Astride her white racing camel, her purple cloak flying, she led her Arab cavalry back and forth across the desert from battle to battle, from victory to victory . . . The world had never before seen such an all-conquering woman warrior.

". . . One story tells that when she heard Palmyra had been destroyed she refused to touch food for thirty days, and killed herself by starvation.

"But another story says Aurelian carried her, very much alive, on to Rome. And there, bound in gold chains, the unhappy Queen was forced to walk behind Aurelian's chariot as he rode through the streets in triumph . . ."

Zeno with William-the-Cat. Trying to figure out what's bothering him. Combing him for fleas. Certain that if she just pays enough attention, he'll convey exactly what's on his mind. In idiomatic English, perhaps. And why not?

Zeno, depressed. By the daily illegal eruptions of no-doubt-poisonous soot from the chimneys of neighboring buildings. By homo sapiens' relentless destruction of loggerhead turtles, the true Ancient Ones. "I'm leaving New York," Zeno tells Flo the night before her twenty-eighth birthday, suddenly afraid she's one of those people who always say they're going to leave New York but never do. Adding, "Winter is my favorite season. The seed beneath the snow."

* * *

The One You're With

*B*ACK IN '64, SOPHOMORE year in high school, she started going out with the Treasurer of the senior class, certainly the handsomest boy around, blond, open faced, co-captain of the basketball team, dapper dresser, avid bargain shopper. He looked like a model in his V-neck tennis sweater, slacks, and saddle shoes; in a bathing suit; in his basketball uniform; in cap and gown and mortarboard, tassel dangling. With classmates he was not so much popular as deemed to possess an appropriate configuration of qualities for political office, but with his teachers there was a real connection. Not because he was an outstanding student, but because he was clean, neat, without adolescent torment, didn't mind giving them "Yes, sir" or "No, ma'am" even though they knew it was hokum.

Vain but remarkably pliable, he generally did whatever she wanted. She loved to tease him about his clothes, his good looks, about being Treasurer but not President or even Vice-President. Actually, his good nature tempted her: sometimes she threw tantrums just to see what he'd do. Or she'd threaten to break up over absolutely nothing at all, stopping abruptly as they began petting, or she'd think of making him pass certain tests, like a fraternity hazing, like a knight pursuing the grail. She'd grin to imagine what the tests should be. Make him go in tux jacket, underpants, and knee socks to his senior prom? Insist he plagiarize a well-known text for English class and then have to talk his way out of it? Her parents had no particular affection for him, but often they told her to stop pushing him around, that the way she spoke to him was "unbecoming." She decided to start making love with him Christmas her senior year, figuring the gossip couldn't hurt since she'd be going away to school, and of course he was already out of state most of the time. Though more than once they'd almost gone all the way, he was surprised when they finally did.

They dated her freshman year of college, and he was a great escort, a good dancer, lots of fun. Dazzled the girls in her dorm. Always in his camelhair overcoat. An ornament. But suddenly, because of the Vietnam war and drugs, people were talking about large or serious or bitter issues all the time, for which he had no appetite. He made a point of presenting himself as a lightweight—"Just out for a good time," he'd say—developing an expertise in golf in 1967, increasingly comfortable with his elders the more his peers seemed headed for confrontation. By the time her first year of college was over she told him she wanted to separate. As she expected, he handled it easily. Their being together had been as convenient for him as for her: she was a beautiful girl, clever, ironic, hip. They'd been compatible, neither of them programmed for sadness.

Her second lover was intense, unreliable, passionate, demanding, and not at all handsome, which squared well with the new aesthetic of the late Sixties. Conventional beauty, like conventional anything, now outré. In 1968, at a Be-In in San Francisco, she met someone who defined the latest status terms for her, a paraplegic who said he was a medium for the spirit of an Egyptian pharoah. The paraplegic had three young women caring for him, all three perhaps also his lovers. Her own lover, without the credentials of such extreme disadvantage, was nevertheless one of the formerly dispossessed— orphan and teenage alcoholic, pachuco cross tattooed on his right hand—which now gave him special entitlements. He also had shoulder-length black hair, a motorcycle, demonstrated against the war, and had earned a black belt in two martial arts. Liked to spar with friends while blindfolded.

As was the mode, she and her lover smoked pot (he'd blow the smoke down her throat as they kissed), went on "food trips" late at night, occasionally headed for Big Sur on his Royal Enfield, roaring down past pumpkin fields on the Coast Highway, racing through the fog at dawn, her arms around his waist, to drop LSD on the beach near Gorda Mountain. They shared a stoned appreciation for all the stars and bizarres the universe kept spinning at them, the plethora of Jesuses and Zorros and Ches, but even so she didn't like it that he was so friendly with other women. "Free love" and, soon, "open marriages" in the air, possessiveness was a no-no, but she was uneasy though he was always "up front" with her, invited her to join him with other lovers or to take her own, though he asserted she was his one and only "ol' lady." Still, she kept feeling she needed him more even as he needed her less. They'd be at a hot springs, or at the beach, and she'd see him naked, the women naked, would start wondering who he'd slept with, who he was thinking of sleeping with. She began "getting paranoid," as they said then, wondering if people were talking about her, fearing he'd leave her, and this went on for six years until, in late 1974, telling her one last time that she was too "uptight," that what he did with other women was just sex and that sex was just another hunger or form of friendship, he moved out.

Single for two weeks, she met a guy who worked in a used record shop, a salesman who said he was really a painter. He was crazy about her. Sent her flowers every day, wrote long love letters, his desire apparently not so much sexual as to have her love, a hunger accompanied from the outset by a terrifying fear of losing her. She knew this was a little strange, but after the previous six years it didn't feel all bad to be pursued. At his insistence, they got married three months after they met, and when her former lover called to offer his congratulations, her new spouse grabbed the phone, began screaming incoherently. At first she was ashamed—how could her husband be so square?—but then it kind of made her laugh. Made her feel good, actually. As her husband shouted at her, "Who says you have to be friends with your former lover?"

At first it was like this, she indulged her husband's insecurity, joked to friends about it, but then he didn't like any of them either, even the women, made it hard for them to visit, write, get in touch. Lost their messages, denied having received the calls, turned the record player up loud when she was on the phone. It was as if anyone she'd known not with him—or just anyone else, actually—represented a threat. If she saw them, his emotional logic seemed to run, then he got less. She'd try to reason with him, since of course there was a kernal of merit in this, but he just couldn't get it when she said that her friends enriched her life. Worse, mention of a former lover or even an event in her past that implied the presence of some former lover her husband construed as a reproach, felt as a wound. Whatever her response—and ridicule had absolutely no effect—he made each interaction with anyone she knew well a battle, was so relentless that she found herself giving up friend after friend without ever quite saying so to herself.

After a couple of years, he quit his job to paint, convinced that if the world recognized true talent he'd soon be famous. Believing in his ability, she told him she'd support them until the Philistines saw the power of his work. In this period, alone all day, he became convinced people were spying on them—

the government, in the form of their neighbors—and, though she first either laughed or was dismayed, after a while she just shrugged, until finally the conspiracy—particularly the coded messages in the daily paper—began to make a certain sense to her. When her parents urged her to see a therapist, she stopped talking to them too. Studied computers after work to be able to help her husband with the lawsuits he'd begun filing, because of which he no longer had time to paint. No matter: he was demanding millions in reparations. Soon they'd be rich and would retire to Hawai'i, if the government didn't asssasinate them first. Sometimes, overwhelmed by the stress of the confrontation, she'd think of turning herself in to the police, though to do so would of course mean betraying her husband.

And so it went until she was thirty-seven. Then one day, having just filed a one hundred page brief in his suit against a radio station he'd accused of harassment by use of subliminal messages on its morning commute show, her husband said, "I think you should have a baby." Long since she'd assumed she never would; he was adamantly against the idea, frequently said a child would only suffer as he had. That the world was too corrupt for a child, would in any case soon end because of nuclear war and pollution. But then, as if in an instant, she was pregnant/her son was born/she stopped working. And as if it was nothing at all, her husband went out and got a job for the first time in seven years.

Their child. Though her husband worked double shifts, came home exhausted, was trying to accumulate enough money for them to make a downpayment on a house, though he loved to hold the baby or just sit watching it, she couldn't shake the feeling that the baby needed all she had, that anything given to her husband was somehow the baby's loss. She began to avoid making love to her husband, though he'd never been very demanding. And on the rare occasion now he did express desire for her, she just let him do what he wanted.

Also, though for one year and then well into another her husband was remarkably stable, never missed a single day at work, she now couldn't escape the sensation that he was in some way not just a rival of but an actual threat to the baby. And this is how it went as their child turned two, as she turned forty. "My man," she'd mutter to her infant son, keeping him very close. "My little man."

* * *

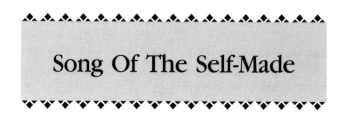

Song Of The Self-Made

*S*ILICON VALLEY, NOT FAR south of San Francisco, only two decades ago still semi-rural, and, back before the orchards and walnut groves, Franciscans and Jesuits vying to alchemize Ohlones into Christians. 'Silicon', however, not like Mississippi/Massachusetts/Susquehana—no shard of an indigenous tongue—but, via Latin, denoting the wafers used in semi-conductors. Valley of the computers.

Not visibly drowning in all this history, Michael at forty-five, Vice-President in charge of appraisals at Golden Northern California County Bank: eighty-seven K per annum plus bonus plus car for the commute. *Ecce* Michael: heading left down the corridor away from his desk, destination a meeting with a V.P. two doors to the right, circumnavigating the entire floor in order to avoid passing the President's office, which, of all the luck, is just next to his. Low profile. Upper middle management. Appropriate strategems, learned by fourth grade, *mit* appropriate disguise—Mr. Middle America, Bay Area style. American flag pin, nice touch, in the lapel of the black pin-stripe suit. Club tie. Think Yiddish/dress British. Suit more stylish than it would be in Peoria, cordovans more expensive, face more lined. Face more lined? Oh, yes, more lived history here in this golden state in the land of the free. Forty-five in '88? Twists and turns. That would make Michael twenty-five in '68: draft eligible/dope-smoking/venereal-disease prone. Traveling around the world on 'liberated' airline tickets when not protesting the war. Right in Johnson's and Nixon's face: one of The People. Selling the occasional lid.

Where have all the flowers gone? Visiting our rawboned democracy in the 1830's, Alexis de Tocqueville observed that where class is not rigidly defined, status becomes an incessant anxiety. *Any* man a king? Though as a revolutionary Michael feared the Thermidorian reaction, was too interested in sex and drugs to be more than intermittently swayed by his own commitments, though he experienced a mean period of living in his car while waiting for some new communal vision to inspire him, by 1971 he'd successfully retooled, quickly enough to be deemed an apostate by radical friends still waiting for the apocalypse. He studied for the real estate broker's exam at a local community college (never did finish the B.A.), took on family in the form of a wife he didn't actually marry and her child by a previous (state-and-church-sanctioned) marriage before they had one of their own. A boy. Glenn with two n's. Accumulating a small paper fortune in the late Seventies' inflationary spiral in housing—no laws in California against realtors speculating—and then losing it when, right in step with the times, Michael developed an interest in cocaine and started milking the properties for cash until interest rates went up, money got tight—he was using his bank cards as a source of credit by then, eighteen percent plus per—and the property was ... gone. All this culminating in bankruptcy proceedings, which turned out not to be as bad as he'd feared.

By then his non-wife wife, heading in a somewhat different direction, had taken up with a victim of the Sixties. Talk about vectors! Here was Michael, aspiring middle class right down to his coke habit after the lost years of civil war and revolutionary dreams. And there was his wife, who though she had no trouble ingesting the coke was nostalgic for some larger freedom, freedom others had tasted while she was stuck raising her first child as a high school principal's spouse, enraged by the inevitability of another day of school for her daughter, another day of school for her husband, another day of obedience classes for the dog, just wanting Something Outside The System. Finally, after long-term passive resistance in the face of Michael's decade of relentless upward mobility, encountering Harry: brilliant but too unstable to work, deeply troubled, living on Social Security. Which is to say, free! Or, she liked coke, but wanted to deal it, not buy it: that way it too would be free.

Meanwhile, coming back one night from their cabin at Muir Beach, traversing Mount Tamalpais, a watershed in the coastal range just north of San Francisco, finishing yet another joint of sinsemilla, Michael crossed a watershed so to speak. "Screw it," he muttered, "she and I are history." Sucking on the roach, he pondered the idiom. *She and I are history.* It suggested, he concluded contemplatively, that he and his non-wife had *become* what they'd once simply been living between them. "That is," Michael said to himself, advancing his line of reasoning, "we are what we were, which, if you think about it, means that now we aren't anything at all." Accelerating down the last section of curves leading to the freeway, taking one last toke, Michael began to laugh. *"All right,"* he shouted, *"All right."*

Not more than several months before this moment, he'd had a true sign. He'd been taking prescription pain medication, had then belted back some Scotch, and was driving the Volvo he'd bought his pregnant non-wife. (Buying a Volvo for the mother-to-be of your child: an apparently inevitable hormonal response for middle-class males.) Michael was in Oakland when he hit the wall. Totaling the car, nearly killing himself. And as the dust settled he'd realized the significance:

he'd *hit the wall*. Decided to put down the drugs/change his life/save his non-marriage, or, as it turned out, cut back on drugs a little and end his non-marriage. Whatever.

In the wake of the accident he also suffered a conversion to a new superego in the form of General Douglas MacArthur. He'd been on MacArthur Boulevard in Oakland when he crashed, you see. Suddenly, in the living room with the red-wood paneling he'd installed at such great cost because of the repose it was to induce, there appeared framed photos—two by three feet—of young MacArthur, all puttees and swagger stick, and soon The General was consulted on Michael's every move. This had to be some kind of a joke, but there Michael was, yet again going into the next room to ask The General's advice in private. And The General's usual response? Well, he tended to point Michael back toward the dreams of the teen-ager Michael had been. Toward West Point. A cadet's life, though in good conscience Michael could never remember whether he'd arrived at the Academy straight out of high school or after coming up through the ranks. The intervening twenty years of national and personal life—total chaos on all fronts—somehow air-brushed away in the process.

Michael in the health club at his stress doctor's behest, staring. Transfixed. A naked old man, checking his hold on the stain-less steel railing, descends into the pool a step at a time. Legs hairless, flesh off-white, breasts enlarged, penis all head and no shaft. Standing waist-deep in the green water, adjusting black goggles and red bathing cap, the old man hyperventi-lates, splashes water on his chest, and then falls forward, beginning an achingly slow crawl, shoulders heaving out of the water each time his head jerks up for air, legs twitching sporadically. Holding on to the edge at the end of each lap for several seconds before again pushing off. "That's OK," Mi-chael tells himself, "only a stickler would call it cheating."

Michael's vantage point on all this? His exercycle. Pedaling in place, he's done two miles, has three to go.

About a mile later he shakes his head, realizes he's been spacing out. The murder of Martin Luther King, his funeral. Corretta King in a pew. Dylan's "All Along the Watchtower," sung by Jimi Hendrix: "There must be some kind of way out of here . . ."

Nearby, some older men are at the Nautilus machines and weight benches. "Yes," comes a voice, "I commuted twenty-five miles each way, two hundred and fifty miles a week, twelve thousand miles a year for twenty-five years. That's . . ."

"Three hundred thousand miles," Michael mutters.

"Three hundred thousand miles," the voice continues.

"He's a self-made man," another voice is saying.

Bell ringing on the exercycle, Michael dismounts and walks past several men who, pedaling furiously while wearing the diaper-like shorts issued by the health club, for a moment appear to Michael to be wizened infants in some kind of tricycle race. Shaking his head, Michael enters the locker room, where Sam is talking about his plans. Same old thing: he and the wife play bridge every evening. Marty, meanwhile, still smarting from being defeated by Sam in raquetball, says he lost because he had sex recently. Sam's rejoinder? "Marty, if you remarry you won't have to worry about that anymore," a line which leaves Michael squinting.

Michael shrugs, composes himself, pulls it all together. Adjusts his tie, slips into a blue blazer. This to round out gray flannel slacks, argyle socks, and sadddle shoes.

Work. After bankruptcy, a period as a free-lance appraiser, dunning clients for checks. Then a headhunter—"my guru," Michael calls him—gets Michael his first job at a bank. A Vietnamese-owned bank, whose directors, having been so kind as to ignore the missing years on Michael's resume, frequently try to get him to "be reasonable before the place goes broke." Michael never fails to hold his ground, but the struggle wears him out, the problem being that a good appraiser should be a kind of in-house cop, challenging loans on property he considers overvalued, the salesmen and, sometimes, upper management, arguing that the appraiser's estimate is too low.

After the Vietnamese-owned bank goes under, the guru finds Michael a position that's more business-like but still not corporate enough for what's proving to be Michael's taste, that is, the new bank lacks the structural dignity and gray hum of layers of employees far removed from any bottom line, a row of elevators to the 17th/29th/38th floor. This though Michael likes being a vice-president, liked it enough to empower his guru to trade two thousand a year in salary for the honorific when his contract was being negotiated. But beyond this Michael wants to manage, not do the task itself, and there are just not enough Indians here. Worse, the company is too entrepreneurial, raw, a one-man show. Of the President and Founder Michael says: "I speak only when spoken to." And, "If you move, he may mistake you for wild game."

Notwithstanding these shortcomings, the job's of course an enormous step forward. By the time he settles into his new office, Michael is sobered only when his guru calls with news he thought Michael should hear from him. "You remember," his guru says, "we were wondering why such a fine position came free. Well, the long and short of it is, your predecessor apparently jumped off the Golden Gate Bridge."

Crazy Davy comes by, throws a rock through the window. In 1966 Davy was going with Anne. Michael slept with Anne a few times, it meant next to nothing to him, Anne had had enough of Davy, but Davy went crazy, so Anne used to let Davy come around as a friend, so Davy got to know Michael. Davy hung around Michael in the antiwar groups, but already seemed to be losing hold. Even his major was all wrong. Psychology in a department of behaviorists, all those experiments on rats, endless journal articles to read, never a book. Then Davy began to smoke dope, but it overwhelmed him, and even behind the dope he wore coat and tie, as if afraid to let the clothes go lest his entire persona disappear, which only made him seem odd to other girls, though Anne seemed to understand. Part of the problem was that Davy's parents were Romanian royalist refugees. Irredentists, never not planning to return the day the Russian tyrants were overthrown. Davy was raised in a suburb, won a varsity letter on the swim team, engaged in heavy petting in his '55 Chevy, but he just couldn't quite get in synch with the land to which his parents had been exiled.

Now, twenty years after losing Anne, Crazy Davy's never put it together. A brief period selling real estate. Small annual guilt stipend from his parents. Some time as a cab driver. Hours every afternoon in the cafes. No girl friends. An occasional impulse to let Michael have it for ruining his life. The occasional call to Michael in the middle of the night, just breathing into the phone. And, once in a while, something more.

When Michael hears the crash, he knows what it is. "Davy," he says to himself, getting out of bed, walking into the living room. Seeing the glass, he heads back to the kitchen for a dustpan and broom.

In the wake of hitting the wall, after The General becomes part of his life, before he meets his wife-wife, Michael solves weekends. He'd always hated them. Vacant, empty, too open to self-criticism. Now, on Sundays, he goes to church. Gets up, gets organized, puts on coat and tie. The only problem being his mother, since he was born and raised a Jew, if of quite secular parents.

"I'm pretty comfortable," he said, after joining a local congregation, the middle-class members' focus less the hereafter than good works in the company of similar others—ecology, women's rights, the homeless. "I'm trying it on, like new clothes. I didn't want to spend the rest of my life as a brunette." Grinning, Michael adds, "The minister's name is Gipper."

Marriage. "Do nothing irrevocable," friends and therapist said when things were going bad with his non-wife. Nonetheless, at a time when Michael was aching for stability she seemed to him to have come up with the analogue of the Symbionese Liberation Army in her friendship with Harry. So it was that ten years after they met, the morning after he crossed Mount Tamalpais, Michael suggested they separate.

A week later, at a realtor's office planning to list his house, Michael started chatting with one of the brokers. Sally: strawberry blonde, going on twenty-seven, never married, bright, straightforward, eager to start a family. "Want to make a deal?" Michael asked her, and she laughed. The next weekend, singing Sinatra—"If you think I'm only foolin' 'bout the French Foreign Legion, think about that uniform with all its charm . . ."—Michael went shopping for an engagement ring. In one store, the proprietor argued that antique rings were no good because they were "worn out," but Michael had a vision of something with history. Also in this period he developed a kind of tic, a chronic manic laugh, as if to say, "I know this seems crazy, but here I am doing it." Or, as Michael acknowledged to his mother, "It kind of takes your breath away." Adding, "but I'm not going to let this opportunity go by." When he phoned with the news he'd begun by saying, "Mom, sit down."

At the wedding, Michael's son by his non-wife was ringbearer, and Gipper, the minister, managed to make no audible reference to Jesus, apparently out of consideration for Michael's mother. Just before the ceremony, Michael inspected himself in the men's room mirror. "It looks like me," he said. "It must be me."

Some years before, Michael decided that TV was the cause of his problems. Too powerful, too many fantasies. Too many simultaneities implying the possibility of participation. Not diverting but confusing. Threatening, actually. One morning, therefore, right after Glenn left for school, turning off the Today Show, feeling both courageous and at risk—he was giving up a way of life—Michael loaded the four sets into his car, drove to a pawnshop in Oakland, and sold them.

When Glenn got home that afternoon he immediately phoned his father at work. "Dad, something happened to all the TVs." Hearing what Michael had done, his son started punching the phone buttons in anger. "Electronic rage," Michael said later, describing Glenn's response.

Learning that his father died when he was nine, Michael's therapist tells him he has no father figure, does nothing to discourage Michael's interest in General MacArthur. Reading Manchester's *American Caesar*, Michael finds that MacArthur all his life tried to measure up to his father's example, that for MacArthur the word "gentleman" had a religious meaning "higher than any title, station, or act of Congress." "Think of it," Michael tells himself, "the humiliation he suffered when they abandoned the Philipines."

As Michael experienced his own life, there was always an enormous amount to forget:

"If the Sixties was a time of judging for me personally, the Seventies was a time of trying to find out who I was as a man and as a human being. And now, in the Eighties, I want action ... without power, nothing is accomplished. The key to power in the Eighties is money, and that was not the key in the Sixties ..."

In the barbershop Michael had picked up a *Playboy*, came

to Jerry Rubin's words, read them, felt tears welling. For the love of God, there he was, waiting for a by-appointment-only haircut, he had a pin-stripe suit/wife/kid/mortgage big enough to crush an elephant. And working in a bank, yes, you made a living, but was it something to boast about, was this the stuff of dreams?

A few days later Michael read an account of the murder of former Congressman Allard Lowenstein by Denis Sweeny. Brave, idealistic, and primed for sacrifice, Sweeny gave all he had to the civil rights movement. By the end of the Sixties, however, he'd become a drifter, sure his life was manipulated by unseen others, feeling enormous guilt for sins only he knew of. Lowenstein, the charismatic left-liberal who'd helped inspire Sweeny, who had perhaps also been his lover years before, was, Sweeny finally concluded, allied with the parties monitoring his mind.

Michael read about Lowenstein's death, Sweeny's madness. He winced: how close he'd come. A Beatles' line occurred to him: "Once there was a way, to get back homeward . . ."

The job. "I love to delegate," Michael says. The joys of delegating undercut only by the President's penchant for humiliating his employees. "Well," Michael says, trying to be positive, "at least they've done away with public hangings."

When Michael married his wife-wife, the question was whether or not to fight for custody of his son. His new spouse understood, he wanted to raise his child, that was a clause in the deal they made, but another part of him wanted never again to see his non-wife or any aspect of her in his son's eyes, mind, spirit. Nonetheless, Michael decided to try, and to his surprise Glenn made it clear to the court that he wanted to live with his father, though the school he'd be attending would be strict and his father's demands about homework severe. Perhaps it had to do with the fact that his mother and Harry were living in a tepee in Ukiah.

One problem was that Michael's wife understandably rued the constant presence of an adolescent not her own, another that because Glenn spent alternate weekends with his mother plans had to be made for the pickups and dropoffs, but Michael's non-wife frequently lost or confused the schedule. Finally Michael installed a separate phone in Glenn's room, said, "I don't want to speak to your mother anymore. You love her, be a good son to her, but otherwise think of me as the quarterback and you're on the offensive line. If the quarterback gets sacked you're on the bench. Up to the tepee."

Passing one year at his father's house and then another, full on into puberty, Glenn developed a terrrible case of acne on his face and back. Having had acne himself, Michael couldn't just stand and watch. So it was that each night he'd apply the medicine to Glenn's back, kept at him about diet and washing and sweating and exercise, went to the therapist with him from time to time to talk about the problems of having a stepmother who wasn't always enchanted with her stepson, Glenn having protected the quarterback very well indeed.

These are words that had once motivated Michael, made him feel he was marching in the Army of the Just:

"... the people of this country must take possession of their lives ... the oppression of any people in the world is our oppression ... the hope for a situation of equality and justice in this country and the world rests on our being free in the face of America."

Inspired, surrounded by thousands of inspired others, Michael heard in his inner ear the soundtrack from *Victory at Sea*.

Though Michael had a gift for knocking girls up in high school

and college, though Glenn was conceived for want of a con-
dom and under the influence of various non-prescription
drugs, Michael and his wife-wife had trouble making a baby.
Which, he soon concluded ruefully, was not the same as
making love. He'd return from work on the given days for
what he called his second job, her temperature having been
taken and taken again, they'd tell Glenn to enjoy a night off
from not doing his homework and go to a movie with the
boys, but month after month there was no good news. They
saw the doctor, learned about hormones/motility/implants/
artificial insemination, spent some weekends off together just
to relax, but when at long last she finally conceived Michael
attributed it to the fact that he'd stopped wearing jockey
shorts.

Meanwhile, in the corridor outside his office one day, Michael stood listening as the President prepared to tell a joke.
"Or are you too busy, Mr. Vice-President-in-charge-of-ap-
praisals?" the President asked. Smiling benignly, all ears, Michael imagined a response: "Excuse me, sir, but can you tell
me how to spell, uh, *wazoo*?"

The President's joke, meanwhile, was about the accountant,
lawyer, and chief appraiser who were being considered for
promotion to CEO. In turn, the board chairman asked each
one to estimate the value of a building the bank was considering financing. To make a long story short, the accountant
behaved as accountants will, crunching lots of numbers in his
estimate, while the lawyer split hairs and cited relevant stat-
utes. As for the chief appraiser—now the President was laughing, could barely get the words out, forcing Michael to make
sounds of appropriate concern—when it was the chief appraiser's turn he walked to the door of the board room,
looked around carefully, and closed it. "And then," the President told Michael, getting a grip on himself, "then the chief
appraiser replied, 'What's the building worth, Mr. Chairman?
In my view it's worth whatever you say it is.' "

Glenn continued to thrive, apart from an incident of streaking while pledging for a high school fraternity. Apprehended by the local police, he ended up volunteering fifteen hours of community service, Michael disturbed less by the offense than by the fact that Glenn was the only boy who got caught. "Point of information," Michael said to his son. "Does naked mean barefoot?"

One evening soon after, Glenn borrowed his father's car. Worried that the emergency brake was still on several minutes after leaving home—"It felt real stiff, Dad," he said subsequently—Glenn pulled the release so hard that it broke. When he came home everyone was asleep, not that he was eager to discuss what had happened, so he went to his room. The next day, about to head to the bank at 6:30, well before the rest of the household roused itself, as usual moving the gear shift to neutral and setting the brake before getting out to raise the garage door, Michael watched the car slowly roll back through the worktable and washer-dryer.

A call from Crazy Davy at three a.m., weird but not too menacing: Davy's version of a bouquet for Michael's impending forty-fifth. Michael's mother in town for the occasion, comfortably housed at his mother-in-law's apartment, the two old moms, as they call themselves, doing fine. Seventeen-year-old Glenn and two-year-old Alice also doing fine. Wife-wife once again very pregnant. With twins, according to the amnio. Homemade carrotcake on the dining room table.

Toupee slightly askew, the gay pianist from down the block plays "Happy Birthday." Beholding the cake, The General standing at parade rest on the wall behind him, Michael smiles, says, "I want to thank my wife, my mother, my friends, my agent...."

"What is this, the Academy Awards?" someone shouts.

Before Michael blows out the candles, he pretends to faint.

* * *

PART II

Public Anatomy

"*P*ART OF MY CURE is interminable waiting," the writer's mother says. She's propped up on pillows on her hospital bed, one tube running into her forearm, another snaking in under the sheet. Hand trembling, knuckles enormous from arthritis, his mother struggles with a piece of the chicken he's cut up for her. Finally she raises the fork, but it begins to tremble and twist; the chicken drops. With insistent control his mother sets the fork back down, as if now it's trying to levitate or escape. "This must be disturbing for you to see," she says.

Brainstem stroke: oxygen-rich blood cut off en route to brain tissue, nerve cells unable to function. Effects slight or severe, temporary or permanent. Over the last few months the writer's come to construe his mother's stroke as a blast of lightning, smells the burn, tastes the ozone. "Will you endorse this check, Mother?" The writer places a pen in her hand. She tries to sign her name, can't. "You're making things too hard for me," she cries. "You're forcing me to struggle with my mind."

In *The Mountain People*, Colin Turbull writes of the Ik, an African tribe in the mountains beyond Lake Rudolf, whom he observed in the early 1970s when their traditional culture was breaking down. Survival of the individual was all; cruelty replaced love; the Ik were mean, greedy, selfish. Children left to fend for themselves, the old abandoned to starve.

The writer also reads an article about a tribe of nomads which in the course of its annual migration encounters a large river. It seems that anyone not an infant has to cross under his own power or be left behind. Thus it happens that an old person is given blankets and food, and sits alone, watching, as the rest of the tribe departs.

Some months after his mother's death, the writer has this dream: he's back at the house where he grew up, which in the dream is where she's died, though of course his parents sold the house years before even his father's death, which itself was more than a decade before hers. In the master bedroom in the dream, in any case, there's the familiar double bed covered with white chenille, chaise longue in the corner, writing desk by the windows, elm trees just outside large and leafy, willows and pond on the far side of the park below. Everything in its place, an Ur reality for the writer, dating from, defining, the very beginning of memory and then confirmed, unchanging, for years and years.

Also in the writer's dream, right in the middle of the room though of course it shouldn't be there, was never there before, is an old trunk with a rounded top—wasn't it in the basement or the attic when he was a child? And now, feeling a sudden surge of anguish, the writer sees that the trunk has been opened by strangers who've gathered around it, who've discovered what the writer and his siblings never knew existed: packets of letters tied in ribbons, diaries with locks on them. His mother's secret life.

The writer comes into the hospital room at a brisk pace, only to be brought up short: the nurses are changing and turning his mother. In an instant the writer averts his eyes, backs out through the doorway, but images are already recorded: zipper of terrible scars on her stomach from the most recent surgery; catheter; thatch of pubic hair.

One doctor, a former pupil of his father's, tells the writer there are many people who simply cannot make themselves go into hospitals to visit family members. The doctor means well, the writer knows, but this idea seems like self-indulgence. Seems like self-indulgence even as he stands in front of the out-patient entrance staring at the electric sliding door, watching it go back and forth again and again as people arrive, depart, as he concludes that each trip inside eats away another crucial quantity of bone marrow.

Up on the ward, the writer stares at the nurses, so young, so healthy, so ready to love, have children, buy a car, find a house, plan a vacation. To go to Filene's Basement, the Cape, Pops, the Bruins. He also plays pick-up basketball on the asphalt court across the street, often with residents and interns he sees on the corridors inside. One of the court regulars is a tall half-Japanese woman from Hawai'i, Michelle, a UPS delivery person, who tells him she had a year on the varsity squad at USC. Whenever possible the writer gets on Michelle's team, frequently passes off to her, both to admire her moves on the court—Michelle can really play, runs effortlessly—and to see her breasts lift as she brings the ball up and over her head before releasing a jump shot.

A week after his mother's death: where has winter gone? Out on the Charles, thirty/fifty/one hundred eight-man shells stroke by, scores of individual sculls. The many runners on the banks are in shorts and T-shirts, spring not only possible but here.

The writer and his friend Paul sit on a bench on the Memori-

al Drive side of the river. Down from Vermont to visit before
the writer heads back West, Paul appraises his old friend's
face. "Middle age comes in on crows' feet," Paul says.

Her dying changes the writer in ways he cannot control.
Whenever he sees an illness or death on the TV news or in a
movie, almost any representation no matter how mawkish,
tears come to his eyes. His mother always howled with deri-
sion at sentimentality, wanted her emotions hard-won, precise. Even when the writer's alone now, his responses embar-
ass him: inadvertently, he looks around to see who's
watching.

After his mother dies he thinks the truth must be told: he'll
do a book of non-fiction on five, ten absolutely ordinary
deaths, the statistically most likely. A quiet book, just spare
portraits of terminal cancer, heart disease, etc., etc. He'll show
people what awaits them. News of the planet: two hundred
thousand people dying per day; seventy million plus per year.

He also begins to shed certain friends and acquaintances.
Almost always, before, he'd been redeemed by irony, could
savor even folly and foible if only for the sake of story. God's
world, such as it was. Now, however, he hears himself passing
judgment all the time, relentlessly, priggishly. He can't stand
it, but there it is. *"Treyfe,"* he often mutters: against all odds,
against his own capacities, he wants it clean.

At a party the writer encounters a professor of comparative
literature he's met once before. In his mid-forties, single, no
children, the professor's defending Rilke against the charge of
narcissism or cannibalism. Rilke was right, the professor says:
he could be "true and fundamental" not by seeking to enrich
the beggar or straighten out the cripple, but only by singing
the "incomparable fate" given them by the "God of complete-
ness."

Suddenly, dizzy with rage, unable to speak, the writer hears the woman beside him begin to respond. "But isn't it being able to celebrate your own suffering that's the real test?" she says, the writer's grimace now transformed into a grin.

"I have to go," the professor says, turning away, the woman who'd spoken then moving toward the table of hors d'oeuvres, leaving the writer staring down a long tunnel in his mind's eye, seeing himself very far down the tunnel, windswept, buffetted, without protection. The sensation that he is greatly threatened, a threat to himself, a threat to others. It also comes to him that he knows this tunnel; with its walls of white tile it's the route under Boston Harbor his family always took to the airport, to the beach. Place and time thus defined, however, the writer experiences no consolation.

In this period an old friend of the writer, now a successful real estate developer, sends the writer—and everyone on his Rolodex—a prospectus for his next project. As the writer reads it, he sees that his friend's biographical summary contains several misrepresentations, minor acts of self-aggrandizement, typical of the man, apparently still and forever beyond his control. Now, however, after years of occasionally pointing out such anomalies or teasing his friend, the writer can't stomach it.

Why? He tries to think it through. To interact with his friend the developer in any way requires complicity in a web of small lies. But this was always true. Time is short? Yes/no/not particularly: he still has a life before him. The writer tries again. "All right. My mother died, this is what's true. Anything false, therefore, attacks not simply The Truth, but *that* truth." He thinks it over. Of course he himself lies, if not as shamelessly as his friend. His mother sometimes lied, the usual social lies. But the sheer number of his friend's lies crosses some threshold, is aggressive, seeks not simply to deter detection but to force compliance. Actively denies, then, the relentless effort at clarity in his mother's writing. More, the goal of his friend's lies is to enhance his vita. It's not just that someone so

determined to inflate credentials is incapable of responding to
the writer's loss. Rather, such voracious promotion of the self
makes it clear the world is going to keep right on turning, with
or without the writer's mother. That the writer's efforts to
remember her or make some claim for remembering her are
nothing in the face of his friend's utterly unstoppable, too-
organic impulse to thrive.

Another man, really just an acquaintance, phones, ex-
presses his condolences, says, "And how are you doing?"
There's an undertone in his question, the writer realizes, that
feels not at all pro forma. And then it comes to him. The
caller's son for years had various problems but seemed finally
to be shaping up. Then one night this son went out for a six-
pack at the local liquor store, was stopped by a robber, and,
though he surrendered his wallet, was shot and killed.

After his mother's death the writer has her books shipped
west. It takes him weeks, but finally he incorporates them into
his bookcases. Her favorites: Gerard Manley Hopkins; Gilbert
White's letters from Selborne; Emily Dickinson; French natu-
ralist Henri Fabre. Her unabridged *Webster's International*,
2nd Edition. A number of volumes on the Puritans. An extraordinary collection of natural history: Audubon, Teale, Austin,
Beston; books on galls and gall insects, the American wood-
cock, animal tools; *Weeds In Winter, Animal Asymmetry, The
Miracle of Flight*.

Going through the books, he finds index card after index
card with words or sentences noted. "Collembola," "fer-de-
lance," "anaclastic," "anaclisis." And, "There is an obvious
resemblance between an unreadable script and a secret
code . . ."

Books finally shelved, the writer clears more space in a
bookcase near his desk. Soon he has Kübler-Ross on death as
the final stage of growth. Stephen Levine's *Who Dies? The
Oxford Book of Death*. This acquisition of books suprises him

not all: just what his mother would have done, what she did whenever a subject caught her interest. On the same shelf, however, he places other books recently acquired: Reik's *Of Love and Lust.* Wilhelm Reich on the Sexual Revolution. *Sex in History,* by Tannahill. Books on various utopian sexual communities. One day he looks over at the shelf, sees the books as if for the first time, starts to laugh. Sex and death.

"I have no more secrets," Ralph says. Married twenty years, Ralph's been a stubborn and truculent husband, often selfish. His wife has seen it all from him. "She knows everything about me, everything. That's hard to live with."

The writer thinks it over. "You know," Ralph continues, "people don't like to talk about this, but there are some losses for which there's simply no consolation." The writer thinks this over too.

After a while, Ralph says, "See, what it is, your parents both dead, now there's nothing between you and the universe."

The writer smiles. Just the kind of hokey statement people can't help making; far less than he'd expect of Ralph. And yet: suddenly the words chill, for a vertiginous split-second he can see it, feel it: the vast, dismaying emptiness of the galaxies, souls of the dead and unborn orbiting the stars, immensity without beginning or end.

At twenty-four, the year the writer's father courted his future wife, seventeen, a freshman in college, he took her to see him perform an autopsy. The corpse turned out to be that of a beautiful little girl. To the writer's mother her future husband seemed radiantly alive as death yielded its secrets. He also took her dancing, but apparently knew only one step, simply kept pivoting her around, around, around until she was dazed, until the music stopped.

After they married, he learned that, having been raised with servants and kept out of the kitchen—her mother was raising opera stars!—his bride had no idea how to cook, and for some time thereafter they often went out for dinner.

They lived in Ghent that first year, always within sound of bells: the very walls resonated, the tuberose begonias in the enclosed garden. Music poured down over them, held in the damp air like drops of moisture. Everything was new and strange, and for that year, alert and seeking, they studied signs, intimations. What *was* the essential Flanders? Carillon? Cobbles? Canal? Pollarded willow?

Nightfall after a day of sleet, lights of rush-hour traffic on Memorial Drive out the hospital room window.

"He does eleemosynary work," the writer's mother is saying, stroke not having eliminated polysyllables, speaking of the husband of a couple whose identity the writer can't place. "Jean and Juan."

"Jean and Juan?"

She grins, as if there's some kind of game in this. "Yes, he does eleemosynary work."

"Eleemosynary work. I guess you're determined to speak charitably of them."

"Very funny."

"Sorry, Mother. You were saying. Jean and Juan."

"Yes. Jean and Juan went to Carthage."

"Carthage?"

"Yes."

"I thought Carthage went out with Gaul."

"You heard what I said."

"Carthage."

"Yes."

"But not Tunisia?"

"I told you. Carthage."

"Jean and Juan."

"Yes."

In early 1974, just thirty, the writer roamed the northwest in a battered '65 Olds Cutlass convertible with the woman he'd fallen in love with, nowhere in particular to go, wandering, wandering. They kept the top down, stopped at one beach, another, studied shorebirds through binoculars, ate in greasy spoons, camped in the fog. During these travels, not having spoken to his mother for a month, the writer called, and in the course of the conversation she told him a neighbor had killed herself.

The writer was standing in a phone booth by the coast highway overlooking the Pacific, not seeing the shape of things to come, the country too damn big, ocean too vast. "I've never really thought about suicide," the writer said to his mother. By then, widowed nearly a year after forty-five years of marriage, she was composing a meditation on the death of the beloved.

"No?" his mother replied. "That's interesting."

Eleven years later, not long after his mother's death, at a time when he came to see that words were inadequate in the face of real loss, that with his parents gone a particular dialogue was now finished, he read something his mother had been working on in that period:

Twenty thousand waves of days
have come over me.
Still not enough for drowning.

Sweets in the writer's childhood: chocolate cakes from Dorothy Muriel's for desert at dinner; Pepperidge Farm cookies in the kitchen cupboard; jars of sourballs and packs of Beeman's chewing gum in the dining room cabinet; Eskimo Pies and Ice Cream Sandwiches in the freezer on the porch. All of this available to the children almost any time, a zone of parental indulgence.

The writer's parents always embraced and kissed whenever

they separated or were reunited, for more than forty years slept in the same bed. His father also always hugged the children whenever he came home from work, whenever one of them was leaving. But as the writer's mother is dying, when his older sister, telling family stories, mentions that they were all breast fed as babies, it starts the writer thinking. Though able to picture his mother sitting on the piano bench beside him, metronome clicking, clicking, as she labors to discipline his playing, though he has no difficulty seeing her sew a button on one of his shirts, ferrying him to school in a rain-storm, pulling off his galoshes, making dinner/washing the dishes/straightening up the house yet another time—all these recurring acts of care, concern, tutelege—the writer can evoke not a single memory of ever being touched by his mother or of seeing her hold or embrace his brother or sisters.

In the early 1970s, after their father died, without comment the writer's sisters began to make a point of embracing their mother whenever they came to visit. Certainly such gestures were a la mode, but his mother, who said not a word about it, never initiated— seemed merely to accept—this physical con-tact. His brother, however, made no such effort, nor did the writer. Thus it was that during what proved to be the last ten years of her life, all through his thirties, the writer would prepare to depart after a visit to Boston, his mother leaning on her cane, walking him from her apartment down the corridor to the elevator. The writer would press the button. After several minutes the doors would open. "Bye, Mother," the writer would say, and he'd be gone.

Sometimes, after her stroke, on the days she's only partly responsive, there are these amazing sudden smiles. Like a baby's, without clear reference to externals seen by adult eyes. Like a mooncalf's. Like the sun popping out from behind a cloud: warming; surprising; blinding.

"You could hurt me," a woman the writer's begun seeing says

several months after his mother's death. "Are you good for me?"

"Speaking as your friend or as your lover?"

"Friend."

"Friend? Well, think of me as the Liberty Bell."

"The Liberty Bell?"

"You know. Free, but cracked."

There's an Armenian man in the emergency room whose ninety-year-old mother has been dying for months. Despite countless death watches, still she survives. Nearly sixty, her youngest son never moved out of the family home. And though at the hospital his siblings come and go, he seems never to leave the waiting room. "He's closest to our mother," one of the brothers tells the writer. "Very close. Never married, never had kids. When she dies he'll get the house. It's only right."

At seventeen the writer went to France, to Grenoble, allegedly to study French, but considered his curriculum fulfilled when he met a Danish girl. She was perhaps twenty. With a directness the writer could not quite forgive, she took him as her lover, and they slept together at her place until the concierge threw her out for having him there. Meanwhile he'd moved out of student housing into an apartment down by the Isere, near the *teleferique.* Madame was German, her first husband a pilot shot down in combat. After the war she learned French by ear, her Monsieur, cross-eyed and very short, a chef she met while he was a sergeant in the French army of occupation.

The writer got to know the family at the *piscine,* helped one of her sons learn to swim, was soon invited to live in the empty bedroom. "Bonjour," Madame would say each morning after knocking, coming through the doorway with a bowl of chocolate and a roll. When the writer told her his Danish friend needed a place, to his astonishment Madame pointed out that of course there was a second bed in his room. Soon she came in each morning with two bowls of chocolate, two rolls, on the tray. Two "Bonjours."

"Mon cheri," Margot wrote him that fall in an air letter mailed to his family home, just before he returned to college, *"je ne suis pas enceinte."* No baby.

Going out to see friends, the writer left the air letter on his bed. Perhaps to take stock of how much of a mess he'd made since coming back from Europe, his mother came up the steep flight of stairs to his attic room, saw the letter on the bed. When he came home that day, walnut-paneled doors were slamming, and his mother was weeping.

"How could you read my letter," he shouted.

"Your father came to me pure," she screamed.

That evening as usual his father returned home from his office at the hospital, but then climbed the attic stairs. Very heavily. Very slowly. It must have been years since he'd come up.

The writer was still crying mad. "Mother shouldn't have read my letter," the writer said to his father, "she had no right," but what he wanted to say was that love and desire seemed in no way synonymous, that long since he wished he'd been kinder to Margot.

He looked at his father, who'd seen so many children die, who was so tired finishing a long day at the hospital after years of struggling with his own chronic illnesses.

"You must stop fighting with your mother," his father said quietly. "She makes mistakes, but she's your mother."

"That's not fair," the writer replied.

His father shook his head, then went slowly, heavily, back down the stairs.

"We all labor against our own cure," his father once wrote,

"for death is the cure of all disease." As a young man he also said to one of his sisters, when she was in a relationship that was breaking her heart, "love unreturned is not love."

That night the writer thought it over. Was it true that his mother was his father's first lover? Did his father really, age twenty-three, come to her "pure"? Did he lie to his future wife? And if he did or didn't, had or hadn't, what of it?

Both because of his father's obligation to help his many younger siblings and the tuberculosis his mother contracted soon after the marriage (enforced quiet at a magic mountain in Switzerland for nine months, then bed rest and pneumo-thorax—collapse of the lung—once a week for many years), they waited until she was thirty to have the first of their four children. By the time the fourth was born she was forty, her husband forty-six. The writer does the arithmetic. They knew each other twelve years before the birth of their first child. Twenty-two years before the birth of their last child. Had known each other forty years when that child turned eighteen.

By the time their first child was born, both its paternal grandparents and its maternal grandfather had died. As for the remaining grandmother—G.—well, the writer's mother never saw her again after her wedding day, though G. lived another thirty-five years. This was not exactly a dark secret in the writer's family, but the subject seldom came up, and only at his mother's initiative. So what did the writer know?

*His grandmother weighed babies during World War I, such community work apparently just the kind of thing she liked. Always organizing people, forming clubs, presiding.

*In 1925 G. took her teenage daughters to Europe for the Grand Tour after pressing her husband to fund the venture, but then for unknown reasons suddenly wanted to get back to the United States, leaving her daughters in London un-chaperoned to complete the itinerary (to shop for snakeskin jackets and crocodile shoes with painfully pointed toes).

*More than once G. came into a daughter's classroom, upbraided the teacher, took her child home.

*As the ship was about to depart with the writer's mother and father on their honeymoon to Europe, there was a fistfight on the dock between his father and one of G's brothers, instigated, apparently, by G.

*Even his mother's sister, a very social being, seldom saw her mother. Whenever G. did visit her mansion in the country, the story went, the household would soon be in chaos, servants fighting with each other.

*Terminally ill, G. came back to Boston. Not having seen her for thirty-five years, after thinking it through—agonizing about it—the writer's mother decided not to go to the hospital.

G. was said to have died berating the student nurse who was caring for her, which the the writer's mother found perfectly in character.

Perhaps the story the writer's mother told most frequently about her childhood—which is to say only four or five times in all over the years—was of taking the streetcar to Symphony Hall with her sister when they both were young. Somehow they lost the fare for the ride home or failed to get the available free transfer. When they finally arrived, having walked all the way back, their mother laughed at them, and, subsequently, if they told her that yes, they could do something, she'd respond, *"I know, I know, Symphony Hall."*

Several months after his mother's death, a former neighbor invites the writer to lunch to celebrate his new book. Afterwards, she walks over to his house with him. Upstairs, under the eaves, they lie on the double bed.

"I'm not myself," the writer says, cat watching them. "I'm crazy."

"I'm married," she replies. "But you know that. What don't you know?"

He laughs. "Where did you grow up?"

"Laredo. Texas. Why?"

"I have a hangup. I can't make love to someone without knowing where they grew up."

"I have some stipulations of my own," she says. "Don't ever call my house. And don't tell anyone."

"Fair enough."

"But you can write about me."

"Thank you. Anything else?"

"I feel guilty."

"There is feeling guilty and there is being alone."

After they make love both are laughing. For him, however, all strong emotions are bound together now: that is, any strong emotion triggers grief. "Hi, Mom," the writer says, like the football players on the sideline when the camera closes in.

She laughs.

"Shhh,' the writer says, "don't wake the children."

"You don't have any children."

"I know."

"You're crazy. I mean it. Really crazy."

"True," the writer says. "True. But I told you that already. I'm just not myself."

A year before her death, the writer's mother, talking with her youngest child, L., her second daughter, keeps bestowing praise on her granddaughter, who at nineteen seems busy being or becoming everything Nana wants in a young woman, everything this child is not, was not. Enthusiastic participation in the mainstream, a positive attitude, apparent compliance with Nana's norms, though once, staying overnight, she invites a date up after her grandmother is asleep. Coming out of a dream, the writer's mother drifts into the living room and sees the two of them on the balcony surveying the river below, embracing until she turns on the living room light and stalks off, waiting for her granddaughter's apology.

Nana and her daughter L. live two thousand miles apart, see

each other rarely but talk every Sunday morning on the phone. Now, during one of L.'s rare visits home, just after Nana once more corrects her pronunciation and asks that in any case she speak up, L. begins to cry, accuses her mother of being endlessly and relentlessly critical. A dutiful child until seventeen, when she went away to college, L.'s never made this kind of outburst before, though it is also true that in nearly twenty years she hasn't spent more than a few days at a time at home.

Later his mother complains to the writer, who's also visting: "Tell me, what does she want me to say? That I love her?"

To love: a verb never used within the family. Too obvious to need being said. To be taken for granted, presumably, after the proof of actions. A given. Tainted by popular overuse. Spurious, commercial, like Mother's Day or Father's Day.

"How are you?" the doctor asks the writer's mother.

"Dreary. What remains to be done?"

"Do you know what day it is?"

"I don't care to know what day it is."

After his mother's death, the writer calls her younger brother, a man of sixty-five, with several questions. "Poor Alfred," his mother always said when referring to him. Alfred, whom the writer's met only once or twice, and not for years: he did not come to see his sister as she was dying, for whatever reason, though they'd always kept in touch. On the phone with the writer, in any case, Alfred is genial, says he'll write back to him, and does. "I regret not being able to provide more information concerning the break between your mother and your grandmother. I was ten years younger than your moth-er—only eight—when the break occurred, and nobody dis-cussed it with me. As I grew up, that rift was something there, done, a fact no one seemed inclined to broach or explain.

"When I was young my mother always seemed very strong,

strong-willed. Unable to go to college for financial reasons, she was determined her children not be deprived. As a result, we three were constantly impelled in a cycle of concerts and lessons—piano, ballet, elocution, singing. Keeping all this in motion took a forceful, organized, capable woman. Suffice to say I don't recall ever having been asked if I wanted these lessons. But that's not so uncommon either, I'd guess."

Back in Boston a year after his mother's death, walking with an acquaintance near Harvard Square, the writer bumps into the physician in charge of his mother's case the last five months of her life, the first time the writer's seen him not in a white lab coat, not inside the hospital. Always, the previous year, the writer and his siblings addressed him as Doctor Haley, referred to him as Doctor Haley when speaking about him with each other, though he was roughly their contemporary. But in his lab coat he evoked their father, no doubt, and perhaps in that context it seemed this surrogate-father had the power to save, or, they wanted to endow him with the power to save.

As the writer registers the thought that in gray slacks, tweed jacket, and cashmere sweater the doctor seems smaller, almost an impostor, the doctor extends a hand to his friend. "Richie Haley here," he says. Startled, the writer remembers that all through his childhood grownups called his father, referred to his father as, Doctor, even his medical colleagues. Now, standing there, hearing the absence of the honorific, the writer acknowledges what he really always knew as his mother was dying: the good doctor is only human.

The writer has a fan, or, a fan for whom he is periodically a fixation. Able to walk only with crutches, she researches the writer's life, learns as much as she can, calls him on the phone, obsesses about him, waits at certain cafes or bookstores hoping to bump into him.

Hearing of his mother's illness, she sends a get-well card, encloses a photo, and writes, "As you might have guessed, I'm most grateful to you for bringing your son into the world."

The writer reads the card to his mother. She's riddled with tubes, is wearing an oxygen mask, vapor condensing on her cheeks.

"Poor thing," his mother says, inhaling heavily, pausing, inhaling again. "But what have I done for her lately?"

"I try to respect her privacy," his mother said. *Respecting your privacy:* the gospel of his childhood. From his mother's *Webster's:* "... State of being apart from the company or observation of others; seclusion ... Private or clandestine circumstances; secrecy ..."

The writer's mother grew up with servants. She'd pass on an anecdote about them once in a while—about May, for instance, who'd chant, "Piss-a-bed, piss-a-bed, hie for shame, the dogs of the country will know your name," who took them to church with her on Sundays—but her essential point about their presence was that all family quarrels were played out before a Greek chorus. The most brazen person, his mother always said—clearly referring to her own mother—would always win.

Privacy. As far as L. was concerned, it meant that for fifteen years her mother did not visit her home. It's true L. was "living with someone," that Nana had no wish to legitimize the relationship by her presence, true that in the last years, travel increasingly difficult, there was much she was content not to have to know out of a kind of fastidiousness. Perhaps also, however, perhaps also she was attempting to give her daughter the gift she herself had never received.

The plane ride back to California after his mother's death. Scrambling out of Harvard Square through the Portuguese and Italian neighborhoods of East Cambridge to avoid rush hour on Storrow Drive, slicing behind MIT, past the Museum of Science, up the ramp by Boston Garden, onto the Southeast Expressway for ten seconds and off again, through Callahan Tunnel to Logan Airport, and then, poof, a lumbering lift-off through the seal of low gray clouds. Heading west, uphill all the way, until at last the jet became one of the many smudges staining the sky south of San Francisco.

Met at the airport by Henry, who'd left Boston in 1966 for what he hoped was the last time to become a freak, a hippie. Born again at thirty-five, Boston suddenly no longer the hundreds of thousands of specifics he'd experienced in a life there—the bleachers in Fenway watching Yaz hit yet another homer; making out in high school on the banks of the Muddy River, hidden in the forsythia—but the "east coast," the dead past. Soon Henry had hair to his shoulders, a button on his peacoat reading *Nirvana Now*. Much of the time he lived in his car, or camped on Jenner Beach studying the seal pods. In this period he also experienced messianic vegetarianism and savored the snares of spiritual materialism when Ram Dass confessed he hadn't really seen stigmata in the palms of a fellow guru (though it did cross Henry's mind that Dass *had* seen the stigmata but *then* chose to lie . . .).

By the Eighties, still in California, Henry was a born-again capitalist, working long hours, complaining about bureaucrats, genially predicting doom—earthquakes off the top of the Richter scale, skin cancer for sunbathers, nuclear winter, stock market meltdown, mass terminal cholesterol. The stress of such threats Henry countered by lying naked on the couch while a (clothed) therapist appraised his 'body armor', Henry's having been developed early with the help of an alcoholic father who abandoned his family. Periodically he'd call to arrange for his son and daughter to meet him downtown for lunch. One time, Henry and his sister took the MTA to Boylston Street and walked over to Jake Wirth's, the old beer hall.

They waited for hours, staring at the sawdust on the floor, but their father never showed up. Never called again.

As for his mother, Henry saw her for the last time as he left Boston in 1966, subsequently spoke with her only rarely. When he learned she'd died, he flew back to Massachusetts, rendezvoused with his sister, went to their mother's apartment. Seeing the terrible disorder, mounds of her personal papers, photographs, and letters, without a word he and his sister began taking load after load down to the incinerator.

So it's Henry who picks the writer up at the airport after his mother's death, as they pass downtown heading onto the Bay Bridge, sky bright blue, not a cloud in sight, tankers lying at anchor waiting for the tide to change. Henry who has transcended the data of his experience in favor of a liberating conclusion, Henry whose intuition his therapist has confirmed, that anything to do with parents is ipso facto pathological.

Autopsy: examination of the self. In 1937, in a text on postmortem examination technique, the writer's father argued that for relatives of the deceased an autopsy is "a form of philanthropy not fully appreciated, and yet possible for people of any economic status," with the additional benefit of "a more complete explanation than is otherwise possible, of the development of the fatal disease ... This may have direct bearing on the health of other members of the family."

Seth, one of his father's many younger brothers. Seth lived with the writer's parents not long after they married, when they returned from Europe. They put him through medical school, gave him the second bedroom in their small apartment. In some ways he functioned as their first child, and though in the world's terms he became a great success, in the family mythology Seth was a fallen angel. The charges against him? Seth left their home without permission, married without notifying them, went West. Went native: in their view failed to measure up to his great potential by surrendering to venal hungers—the desire for money and political power, the need to impress. Later, Seth also divorced. All through his childhood the writer identified with Seth; his parents' categorical criticism seemed to a recalcitrant and oft-disciplined child to suggest failure on their part, unacknowledged truths. The writer was disabused only when, turning twenty, on his first trip to California, he encountered his uncle. It was a living lesson in genetics, how similar and yet how unlike each other siblings could be: he saw aspects of his father in his uncle's every gesture or word, but as in a funhouse mirror.

Now, after his mother's death, the writer calls Seth. After they chat for several minutes, Seth says that the writer's father was a genius but modest, then quickly implies he himself's that kind of a man. This he follows with a joke about the fellow with the long beard in the nudist camp. "Somebody has to be able to go to the store" the punch line, all to set the writer at ease, presumably.

Finally the writer is able to ask what it was like to live with his parents so many years before. "You have to remember," his uncle says, "your mother already had tuberculosis when your father met her. The white plague. One of its symptoms is extreme irritability in the early stages. She was beautiful, brilliant, impatient. Very, very demanding of others, including me. She was the apple of your grandfather's eye, and he must have been wondering who'd take on and protect a headstrong girl with so much ability. Your father was the answer to his prayers. Your grandfather could see they'd be like swans, mated for as long as they lived. He encouraged the marriage, which itself was enough to make his wife G. hate your father. Anyway, she and your mother were already fighting all the time. Your grandmother wanted to run your mother's life, but no one was going to do that."

"What are *you* doing here?" his mother says as the writer comes into the hospital room.

Several months after his mother's death the writer meets Carol. Twenty-two, from Salt Lake—stress on Salt, she explains—father a Mormon businessman. Having come to San Francisco, she's repudiated her childhood role models, all her girl friends from high school long since married with children. Though clearly bound into the family romance, she has little good to say about her parents. Just barely, the writer stops himself from admonishing her to cherish them. When they make love she's so young, so healthy, so tough in her determination to carve out her own life that the writer thinks of the Beatles line, "She's the kind of girl you want so much it makes you sorry."

Carol's often frowning, thinking things through, has cropped her hair, wears long earrings, is independent, cool. Because she's a dancer, they go to see a thin update of *West Side Story,* which seems to absorb her completely. As the on-screen action moves to Spanish Harlem, the writer leans over to her. Despite the verve of the break-dance sequences, something in the film's banal plot is making him terribly lonely. "I used to be Puerto Rican," he whispers, but she just shrugs.

"See you," Carol calls out as she prepares to leave the next morning. How can she know that all change, anything like a disappearance, leaves him splayed?

"What does that mean?"

"What?"

" 'See you.' "

Carol turns as she reaches the door. "It's just a phrase," she says.

The writer searches, checks with his siblings. No, no pictures of his parents' wedding, nor can they remember ever seeing any. Further, no pictures of their mother's parents, either one.

Even on the days she's feeling stronger, the writer's mother finds it hard to speak on the phone, and visitors just overwhelm. The writer stops by the nearby house of one of his mother's old friends, accordingly, to report on her condition. Already past eighty, this woman is still quite articulate, vital, undaunted.

After they speak about his mother's prognosis, her friend tells him that several years earlier she'd been in a coma for ten months. Laughing, she says that everyone gave up on her. "Good thing they didn't bet their lives on it," she adds, because one day she simply woke up, was once more back in the world. She shrugs.

Her story: told without a sense that she felt any particular stake in its outcome. Without a hint of information about the Other Side. Without at all suggesting the writer's mother will have the same roll of the dice.

The writer asks his aunt, his mother's sister: "Why was it always 'Poor Alfred,' that my mother said when referring to him? What was the problem?"

His aunt cackles. Once an extraordinarily beautiful woman, a model, actress, star in musical comedy, she's bent, wizened, seems to be wearing a wig a la Louis XIV. "Alfred," she says. "A successful doctor, four healthy children, etc. etc. All very fine, very fine. But your grandmother made him live at home during college. She didn't want him to have dates, go to parties. Your mother and I escaped early. Your grandmother wasn't about to let that happen a third time. She wanted to engineer poor Alfred's marriage, and she did." She pauses. "Though who knows, perhaps it was all for the best."

After a setback, his mother cannot feed herself, lacks sufficient arm strength to lift the fork. At the same time, her thinking is again quite coherent, a great relief to her children: she seems once more 'herself.' The writer and his mother speak of one of her acquaintances. "I marvel," his mother begins, "but mind you, she's done quite well with what she has," and they both grin at the calumny of such faint praise.

Several moments later, the orderly brings in dinner, and the writer begins to help his mother eat. A bite at a time, bite after bite, until he is certain they'd both prefer the nurse do it from now on.

There's a picture of the writer's mother taken perhaps a year before her stroke. She's looking right at the camera, waiting calmly, on her lips just the hint of a smile. She knows what she knows, offfering in the biographical note for a new book that during her life she's portrayed wife/mother/widow/grand-mother, considers these characterizations her leading roles, has in addition enacted actress/singer/poet/translator. She also plays the eccentric grande dame, reserving the right to speak in her own idiom. "I'll be there presently," she says, accent ever more mid-Atlantic.

Age seventy-two, in many ways she's beyond obligation, though she well knows the ambiguities of what she calls "an almost frightening freedom":

... nobody's made me cry in years.

(I miss the hug coming after the tears.)

In her life as a widow, little left to lose, there's writing and its cool clarity, the solitude she loves, and readings/concerts/performances. These various removes she'd always sought, the discipline of Art and its pellucid passions, some saving distance from the noisy chaos of life.

Though never explicitly stated, it was the writer's father's vision that his children would help each other and care for his wife after he died, and in fact they did just this, though as they grew up it was simultaneously if seldom acknowledged that their mother never saw her mother again after age eighteen, that their father's younger brother was persona non grata, that with relatives there were always inevitable hard choices to be made. Even so, the children fulfilled their father's unspoken wish despite the usual good reasons to the contrary. The writer's older sister, for instance, liked people, loved to dance, dated earlier and more than her mother approved of. By the time she was twenty her parents had broken off a number of her relationships: the sailor she went out with in high school, the dancer she met in Mexico after freshman year of college, a medical student whose tenure ended when they were discovered 'making out' in the living room late one evening. Her senior year of college she married a man one of whose principal virtues was that he had no trouble at all—perhaps even enjoyed—standing up to her parents.

Survivors' tales. The writer's mother loved them, dealt with them in poetry again and again in the years after her husband's death. Her most powerful, perhaps, being a solution to the tomenting question of what happened to the innocent left-behind beasts after Noah loaded up the two-by-two and sailed off. In *her* version—rejoice! rejoice!—no living thing was lost.

His mother lies there, eyes intermittently open, occasionally raising her eyebrows as if in response to something said, but not speaking. Playing possum? "She's had a tough course," the nurse says.

The clouds are low, gray, without hope: Boston as Prague. Silent, inscrutable, his mother's become a Rorschach test, open to speculation, withheld response awakening all the primary conflicts. The writer begins to cry. "You're a good son," the woman at the reception desk says as he leaves.

Though he's utterly lost, the writer time and again refrains from trying to patch things up with his former wife. It was only after they separated that she told him, the first time ever, he thought, that she loved him. Actually, what she said was, "You know I've always loved you."

One night, up late, he remembers the first time she came to Boston with him. They were still just wandering, staying in friends' apartments, heading down to Nantucket in the middle of winter, out to the Berkshires, back into the city. Finally they went to have her meet his mother, who commenced an interrogation as soon as they were seated, sherry and cheese on the low table in front of the living room sofa. The writer's wife-to-be, then twenty-two, answered several peremptory questions—about family, college, plans for the future—but finally, clearly making a decision, began to respond more and more softly, until she was nearly inaudible and then, smiling politely, ceased to answer his mother at all.

As the writer grew up there were very few adult visitors to his parents' home: never a party, no overnight guests, someone for dinner only rarely, no clan gatherings. There were a number of reasons for this. To begin with, his father was working at the hospital nearly every day of the week, seldom coming home until evening. Parties just didn't much interest him, nor did he have any desire to rise socially: he was doing what he loved. Entertaining colleagues he could take care of at lunches at the hospital. As for family, his wife had long since cut herself off from most of her relatives, and the weight of his many siblings led over time to a policy of distance where possible. Phoning rather than visiting. There were stories about the early years of marriage, the writer's mother singing lieder at Sunday afternoon receptions, but this was long in the past. Now there was generally only Richie, Jonah the Tailor's hapless son-in-law and delivery man, who always seemed to be leering at the writer's mother, to be trying to invent a reason to get into the house, the writer's mother just as persistently, year after year, telling Richie through the kitchen window and storm window to just leave things on the porch.

Occasionally one of his father's foreign counterparts—an Englishman, a Swede—or one taciturn and saturnine American doctor, a man of enormous integrity, would come for sherry. The writer and his siblings would sit with their father and the guest in the music room, making conversation, and then, suddenly, his father would say, "Ah, there she is," and their mother—hours of cleaning house behind her—would come sweeping down the stairs as they all rose. Just once, his mother tried to draw out the laconic American doctor, waxing rhapsodic when he said he'd grown up in Vermont in the Depression, asking what it had been like. "Outhouses, no plumbing, a well, the runs every spring," the doctor replied.

There was also the writer's trumpet teacher, perhaps thirty when the writer was fifteen. His mother then in her late forties. Following years of lessons, the writer and his teacher had passed to a quasi-collegial relationship: after a rehearsal or weekend Pops concert his teacher would stop at the house and they'd work on duets together, his teacher no longer accepting payment. Each time, after they'd played for a while, sitting in front of the music stand with the enormous Clarke bible of trumpet exercises in front of them, they'd hear the French doors start to open and his mother would appear. His teacher, Italian from New Orleans, with an easy smile and southern accent, would nod his head and courteously respond to her questions, though he never initiated any exchange. Nor did he rise when she came in, though clearly this was her unspoken expectation. "Demand," his teacher might have termed it, had he not been far too gallant to bring up the subject.

The writer's Uncle Hugh, huband of his mother's sister. When he married Hugh was already a high roller, always a deal on the horizon, servants, limousines. At his mansion, ice cream for kids was brought in by the cook, flambé. "I can't see why you want to know about your grandmother anyway." Hugh's never had children, and, more germane, has a problem with information. Age seventy-five, having dedicated himself for years to advancing in 'Society'—endless charity balls, frequent dinner parties, a regular at "21"—he's recently been indicted for fraud.

"No big deal," the writer replies, "we just want to know."

"It's really simple," Hugh says. "Your grandmother G. wanted her daughters to marry better men. Nobody was good enough. She wasn't interested in promise, of which your father obviously had an unlimited amount; she wanted social cachet. I had to date her daughter in secrecy. Friends of mine would take her out, then meet me at the Copley Plaza. Your mother would have known all about this. At seventeen she must have decided her mother could threaten her marriage. Your grandmother already ran her relatives' families, was a real power broker. Later, when Alfred was older, she controlled his social life. He was like his father, easy going, would go to great lengths not to fight."

Hugh coughs, pauses. "Anything else?"

"No. Thanks, Hugh. That really helps."

"Oh, I'll tell you something," Hugh says. "One day, when you children were still very young, your grandmother decided to try to see you. She never had, of course. Apparently she went to that beautiful park across from your house and sat there and waited and waited until she saw you come out. Then she just watched while you played, until you children went back in."

What Hugh didn't tell the writer was that when Hugh was twenty, his aunt eighteen, that is, several years before their marriage in Boston, they secretly married up in Vermont. Their license to make love, or to make love without fear. The writer wonders. Did his mother know then about the secret marriage? Did she know her older sister was sleeping with

Hugh? Did G. know? Was that part of her vendetta against her second daughter's fiancé, the fear or knowledge that they were sleeping together? Was that the source of her rage? Or did she really believe he was after their money? Sex, money: wouldn't it have been with an accusation about one or the other that she went to see his father's mentor, a very famous professor, to vilify the talented young physician who wanted to marry her not-yet-eighteen-year-old?

"Wie Geht's, Mother," the writer says as he enters the hospital room.

"Ganz gut. I saw Victor," she replies, speaking of one of her dead husband's many brothers.

"You did?" Uncle Victor is 3,000 miles away, she'd spoken with him on the phone earlier. Her son had dialed the number.

"Yes. Victor looked very well."

"Believing is seeing, Mother" the writer responds, and she cackles.

"Are you promiscuous?" Ana asks. They're in North Beach, wandering past a playground after Haka Chinese food, watching Chinese kids shooting hoops, playing softball. She doesn't wait for an answer. "I've never done this before," she says later as they get in her car, referring to the fact that they're on their first date. As they drive across the city he thinks of the the question behind her statement: "But have you?" And hears the response from the song: "Well yes I have/but only a time or two . . ."

When he wakes up at her place the room is pitch black, only flashing red numerals on the electric clock for illumination. Her mother committed suicide/her father died young/ she believes in psychiatry/her hair is red and short/she has very blue eyes/she calls herself an introvert/she doesn't like her sister/she likes his shoulders. She believes there should be a university for love, so people can learn how. Had said to him, "I'm old-fashioned."

When she wakes in the morning Ana asks, "Did you turn the hall light on?"

"Yes. Around two this morning."

"Why?"

"I've had one on at night since my mother died."

"Why?"

"I just have."

"But why?"

"Well, otherwise I might get lost."

"How?"

"I guess I wouldn't be able to get back."

"Back where?"

"I don't know. Just back."

The writer's father had an older brother who was studying philosophy in Germany. This would be in 1921 or 1922. Finishing college, the writer's father went over to join him, his goal to study with Sigmund Freud (who'd come to the United States in 1912 to deliver lectures at Clark University). When he reached Freiburg, however, he was incorrectly informed that he needed to be a physician to become an analyst—Freud was by then bitterly opposed to the scientific establishment—and so began medical school. Soon, encountering a great teacher, he became intrigued with pathology, over the years growing increasingly skeptical of pyschoanalytic models.

The writer's mother intensely disliked psychiatry and psychiatrists, though she never quite explained why. When, as an adolescent, the writer became enamoured of Freud, his mother bristled. What, the writer—teenage specialist in perceiving the latent, in detecting the unconscious—used to think, what was she so afraid of?

His mother's poetry. Dense. Elliptical. Nothing simple revealed, or, nothing simply revealed. At seventy-three, however, she publishes a first novel in the form of a diary of a seventeenth-century teenage girl whose parents are killed by Indians and who, kidnapped by them, is finally ransomed by whites in Boston. Working as a servant, the girl is then possessed by spirits and exorcised by the twenty-nine-year-old minister Cotton Mather. There's some laying on of hands involved in the cure.

Appraising his mother's transition to prose so late in her career, the writer supposes she was expressing both an impulse to be more explicit—and about some things more accountable, therefore?—as well as an interest in confronting the sexual element of a teenage girl's life. Not only do Mather and the girl have an intense and erotic—if technically chaste—relationship, but the girl, it turns out, had become pregnant while with the Indians. And in the sequel his mother was planning just before her stroke, the girl, as in the historical record, is drummed out of Mather's congregation some time after her exorcism—for adultery.

Not long before her death, his mother wrote a poem to celebrate the christening of the child of two lesbian acquaintances. Her own children were amazed. Wasn't this condoning just the kind of "inappropriate" behavior she'd long enjoyed deploring? Ten years past the death of her husband, having had to redefine her relationship to the wider world or be alone, their mother hooted, laughed, professed to think nothing of it.

Assaults of the hospital: grinding routine, harried personnel. A nurse impatient with the writer's mother, whose oxygen mask has slipped off yet again. "She's moving around too much," the nurse says testily.

The writer feels his mother waiting for his response. Weeks passing, the hospital world ever more total, at the mercy of so much expertise, both of them increasingly lose autonomy, feel infantilized, become co-conspirators against the quasi-parental hospital authorities.

"You know," the writer finally says to the nurse, "believe it or not, before I was born I asked for a mother who would move around too much while wearing an oxygen mask in the process of recovering from a stroke at age seventy-four."

Putting the mask back in place, his mother's one good eye staring up at her, the nurse replies, "You asked for it? You got it."

Inez. Twenty-one, a Philipina, just finishing college and working as a receptionist in a doctor's office. Hoping to get a M.A. in public health sometime, but for now dreaming of getting out of her mother's house. Saving every penny.

What she likes about the writer is that he's not trying to be her lover, so she wants him to be her lover, so he becomes her lover. She stops by his house, and he listens as, like Adam, she names the things she sees. This skylight, that white wall, those Spanish tiles.

For several months she visits once a week or so. She's wise: "This is just what it is," she tells him.

Neil's concerned about the writer. "I don't know how you do it," he says, meaning living alone, flying back and forth cross country since his mother's stroke, spending day after day at the hospital when it's his turn to alternate with his siblings. The writer and Neil have worked together in the past, but just now the world of getting things done seems incredibly remote. Not unwelcome: beyond reach. As if he and his siblings are also consumed by their mother's stroke.

Neil perennially worries about everything, sees all the dangers, wants the writer to draw the proper inferences. How can he not be raising a family? "I mean, come on, stop bullshitting yourself," Neil says. "Think about it. Look who's taking care of your mother."

"Make your soft palate like the skin of a drum. Calm, calm, calm. Have the sensation of each note coming towards you, not moving away. Start the sound from the ears backward, tongue wide at the sides. Make your throat like a cobweb: the vowel is the fly caught in the cobweb. To sing one must be an actor. Never be yourself when singing."

The education the writer's mother and her sister received, another element of which was the study of elocution and appropriate gestures. They'd recite: "The hand defines or it indicates. It affirms or it denies. It accepts or it rejects. It molds or it detects." Or they'd go through the catalog: *Arms*—Declaration, Negation, Rejection, Appelation, Benediction, Salutation; *Feet*—Defiance, Respect, Vulgar Ease, Indecision. Or they'd declaim once again: The prophet reveals mystically/ The saint reveals spiritually ... Oh, play on the light lute of love, blow the loud trumpet of war ...

The writer's mother and her sister were forever being taken to the symphony, vaudeville, concerts. "If Pavlova stood still it was breathtaking," the writer's aunt told him. "She was the dying swan. Also, wearing a yellow satin dress, she did a gavotte to music by Galinke. Your mother and I went backstage. We were impressed that she didn't shave under her arms.

"We saw Isadora Duncan dance too. She ripped open her costume, exposed one breast. 'This,' she said, '*this* is beauty.' But we weren't impressed, we were brought up in the Russian Ballet. We were always in tutus, like in the Degas paintings. Our teacher was a White Russian refugee. She was nearsighted, wore a lorgnette studded with jewels. She had a baton, would bang your legs. Our toe shoes were always full of blood.

"We did a ballet at the home of Mrs. Arthur Curtis James at Newport. They had a Swiss village in the rose garden. Your mother was an oriental rose. Later there was ballroom dancing, with many White Russian refugees. God, they waltzed magnificently."

The writer's aunt coughs, chokes, recovers. She's chain-smoked for since she was eighteen, since before the ballet at Mrs. Arthur Curtis James'. More, she's got a husband in legal trouble, enormous debts, social stigma. "If your mother were alive," she tells the writer, "oh, if your mother were alive, she'd have me come to her."

Revived by the thought, his aunt begins to recite from *A Midsummer Night's Dream*, lines she and her sister learned more than fifty years before. "How now, proud Titania!" his aunt declaims. And, "Lord, what fools these mortals be."

The writer's friend Felicity, whose mother, leaving a love child with her parents, ran off from a small Mormon town in the '30s. Whose mother was later found dead in San Francisco, a suicide. Felicity herself running off fifteen years later.

Inhaling deeply on her cigarette, Felicity studies the writer as if to read the effect of the death of a second parent. "You know," she finally tells him, "they say that if you're an orphan, you grieve the whole rest of your life."

The writer chews on it. Two thoughts recur:

1. How could their mother abandon her four children after demanding so much of them?

2. How would they now be able to explain why they were the way they were?

His mother begins to vomit, almost chokes to death before the nurse can clear her throat, insert nasal tubes to empty her stomach of fluids. Later, after the writer's brother comes in, his mother finally opens her eyes. "How could you let them do that?" she asks him. "How could you be so cruel?"

Some children and their teacher from a local private school plan a book on dying, come to speak to the writer's mother. "What are we interviewing her about?" the teacher asks as the tape begins to run.

"Death," says a student's voice.

"Fire away," his mother responds.

When they ask if she's afraid of dying, she says, "I don't think so. I feel I have led a rich life, a life of achievement. Though my work, my writing, still engages me, you reach a point, with gradual curtailments, when the prospect of continuing just isn't that interesting. I don't need more; that doesn't seem frightening. I do hope for a graceful conclusion. I want to accomodate myself to what I see in nature. Once was enough . . ."

Neither of the writer's parents has a grave. No gravestone, either. Nor can the writer remember any conversation with his parents, ever, about the hereafter, pro or con. It was apparently just not a subject of great interest to them. Asked by the high school students writing about dying what thoughts she had on afterlife, his mother says, "I abstain, though I must say I really don't expect any emanations from the unknown."

His parents died within a week of each other, eleven years apart. Some winters, season winding down, spring on the way, the writer remembers the anniversaries of his parents' deaths only by accident. Or, more precisely, he begins to feel uncomfortable in late March, wonders what's eating him, suddenly realizes it's the week of the anniversary of his mother's death, his father's soon to follow.

Regarding what happens to someone after death: as his mother noted, Frost wrote, "Strongly spent is synonymous with kept." And Ezra Pound, she observed, said, "What thou lovest well, shall not be reft from thee." Beyond this, the writer inherits among his mother's unpublished papers her meditation on the continuity of matter, her "search for what cannot be taken from me, that this love happened," her thesis that the death of the beloved results in a dispersal—but not loss—of essence akin to the sudden scattering of a flock of birds. "To take pleasure in dissolution," she wrote, "as one enjoys beholding the dissolving shapes of clouds." Or loss, she posits, as a circling. Loss as reversible. Going forward into the past. Loss not unreturning infinity but circular renewal, as of the seasons. "With the help of metaphors" she wrote, playing the wind-lasser, "I lift your loss on board." Of course she would confront the death of her husband, transfigure it, in art. As she wrote, "O love, my other wing."

Again the writer's aunt. "It was typical of my mother G. to engineer deals that couldn't possibly come through. Your mother was to become a singer, that's what all the lessons were for, though she could have been a dancer too, but then my father finally learned of all this and said no. No one had ever mentioned it to him.

"My mother would talk to your friends, or teachers, without you knowing. Once, while my husband was in the army during the war, she suggested I get in touch with my old beaus, actively encouraged me.

"It was always nervewracking when my mother visited. Constant trouble. You wonder about these genes . . .

"She caused the tuberculosis your mother got. She killed my father. He died of heartbreak after your mother's marriage, after the rift. My mother got a thing against your father, though she should have been thrilled. She accused your father of horrible, horrible things. It must have been terrible for him. Your mother was afraid her marriage would be destroyed.

"My mother was the type who appeared suddenly. She'd interfere with everything. My father, just to have peace, let her get away with most of it. My mother was very unusual. They've discovered more now. Perhaps now they have some medicine."

His aunt sends the writer a book, *Farinelli, Le Chanteur Du Roi.* As she says on the phone, "Farinelli was the most famous castrato of all time. He spent twelve years in the court of Spain, singing to the mentally disturbed King Philip every night. When Carlos III succeeded Philip, however, he banished Farinelli, saying, 'I don't like capon.' "

The writer's dying aunt, her obsession with Farinelli, her belated discoveries about her husband's frauds now that they no longer have the money to heat, much less repair, the mansion: what to make of her version of the past?

The writer and his younger sister were back in Boston for a visit, talking with their mother about the houses she'd lived in, and suddenly there they were, the first time ever, heading over to Franklin Park to see the house she grew up in until her parents took the next immigrant jump of upward mobility. This house now in a black ghetto, the grape arbor of her childhood still in the yard. "My mother," she once wrote, "building me in/to my body, bolted me secure/and gave me freedom of a house./ . . . Mother! Mother! I cried,/I'd give my house for a key/to free me from my house!" Letting down her hair, she "gave out a hand to the climber/coming over the sill . . ."

The house in Roxbury. Odd, actually, that the writer and his sister ever did make the trip with their mother, so unsentimental about the past did she seem. So little past did she appear to have, almost none at all predating her marriage. Perhaps, however, her past was always like the house. Very close by, all too easy to get to.

Turning twenty, the writer left Boston, headed west, was for years pulled back again and again—no other place would ever feel so specific, so true—but always once more he went away, in large part to be free to invent himself. His mother, however, lived in Boston seventy-one of her seventy-four years, spent much of her adult life no more than several miles from where she was raised. Had to fight right there for all she had: nothing was going to just be left behind.

"We are molded by those who love us," writes Anatole Broyard, "those who refuse to love us. We become their work, one they don't recognize, not what they intended . . ."

"Am I improving?" his mother asks.
 "Do I look any stronger?"
 "I want to maintain my independence."
 "I'm afraid you'll stop taking me seriously."

The family geneologist, nephew of the writer's grandmother, answers his call. "Yes," he says, "your mother's mother would come to Boston every year to stay at the Copley Square Hotel. Not the Copley Plaza, mind you: this was a more modest establishment. In any case, your grandmother was one of the most colorful characters in my experience. A very commanding presence. She used to hold court. My parents were good listeners. She alway talked with lots of exclamation points. Spoke about her grandchildren—you people, I mean—as if she saw you regularly, was just bringing us up to date."

Post-mortems. (As James McConkey puts it, "The dead are at the mercy of the living.") From his mother's manuscript, her meditation on the death of beloved: "The pathologist has sent me this autopsy report. "Your terminal episode was probably an arrhythmia, or a very recent extension of your infarction."
 Heart (680 grams):
 Right Atrium—Dilation and Hypertrophy, Moderate
 Right Ventricle—Hypertrophy (0.3-0.5 cm.), Dilation, Moderate, Focal Fibrosis
 Left Atrium—Dilation and Hypertrophy, Moderate

Left Ventricle—Hypertrophy (1.5 cm.) and Dilation. Old Healed Infarctions, Anteroseptal and Posterolateral (5x4 cm. and 9x7 cm. Respectively) Continuing her dialogue with the beloved, his mother writes, "Whatever you were, you are no longer. This is the message of the funerary theatre."

She then refers to the Dutch anatomies of the Renaissance. Public invited, seating according to social rank as cadavers of the criminal and unfit were dissected: " 'Only humble and unknown persons, then, and those from distant regions may rightly be claimed for dissection, that there shall be no outrage to neighbors or relatives . . . neither lean nor fat, and of rather large frame, that their components may be of more generous size and more distinctly visible to the onlookers . . .' " Questions from the audience were admissable, provided they were serious.

Going back through his mother's books, the writer locates William Hecksher's study of Rembrandt's *Anatomy of Dr. Tulp.* "The portrait as an art form," Hecksher writes, "is from the beginning closely linked with the idea of death," Rembrandt thus in the role of recording angel. Of the luminaries of Amsterdam seen in Rembrandt's painting, Hecksher argues that they "sought immortality when they commissioned Rembrandt to represent them for all times to come as a group in contemplation of death, of its various causes and effects, of its physiological and its moral aspects. Naturally such reflections would simultaneously lead to a deeper understanding of the phenomenon of life itself." Beyond this, there was in the public dismemberment of criminals the element of further punishment, such atonement cathartic for the audience, though some contemporaries deplored this blend of science, retribution, and spectacle: " 'Antiquity knew not these torture chambers . . . where these unnecessary cruelties are practised by the living upon the dead.' "

His mother's highrise. Just downriver from the hospital, a world of its own. His mother so close and yet so far, the life of the building goes right on. The super expediting somebody's possessions in, somebody's out, one of the elevators draped in mover's blankets. Residents headed to the basement with laundry. Concierge holding a package at the desk, forwarding a message, asking for news of his mother's condition.

His mother's apartment, the two hundred and seventy degree view she described in poems so many times. Oarsmen, joggers, setting sun, Larz Anderson Bridge, steeples, smokestacks, rising moon, rush hour traffic, gull/mallard/pigeon, skyscrapers downtown and the radar tower at Logan Airport, lovers on the river banks below caught in the "sometimes prurient lens" of her binoculars.

Her apartment, where she hung on for dear life after her husband died, until art and irony—whew—clicked back in. Then staying put, not simply self-protection but a form of fidelity. Sycamore, ailanthus, ash, apple, cherry, larch, dogwood, aster, willow, copper beech, Chinese maple, all as seen from above; snowfall of migrating moths blown up in a storm; crimson champleve beetle on the balcony railing; three dollars' worth of ladybugs to rid the podocarpus of aphids. The local and quite precise variety that sustained. As she wrote:
. . . Why should I travel? Where else would I be?
Dream is my distance and it comes to me.

"Where are you staying?" his mother asks the writer not long after her stroke, meaning, "Not in my apartment, are you?" But where else can they/should they stay, it's for her they've come. Even so, they understand her feeling of displacement, loss of control.

As weeks become months, as the four of them return to the apartment time after time from their own homes, it seems increasingly less hers, precise shipboard packing away of things slowly undone, accumulation of tiny changes accruing to new essence. Not the same brand of soap or toilet paper, book replaced on a different shelf, a plant dying, coffee spilled. Of course they try to be careful, but often, witnessing the net effect of their presence, they feel like vandals. One night, back from the hospital next door after trying to cheer his mother up before she undergoes yet another operation, the writer has a sudden desperate craving for chocolate, ransacks the kitchen drawers, finally finds the boxes of after-dinner mints in the liquor cabinet. Eats them, all four boxes. Pours himself a Scotch, then another. Starts taking hits from the bottle.

In the morning, surveying the wreckage, thinking of *A Clockwork Orange*, he begins to clean up, and then, taking in the magnitude of the task, all the daily maintenance that has not been done the last few months, makes several phone calls. Soon, not a cleaning person but a cleaning crew arrives to work at a dizzying pace, a total of ten man-and-woman hours performed in two and a half, and when they are done, gear back out in the hall near the elevator, writer signing a check, the apartment is spotless. Spotless, but now even less his mother's, every chair/sofa/table slightly off the mark, each piece of bric-a-brac or *objet d'art* at a new angle.

Taking stock of this transformation, the writer also begins to see that though the apartment has a beautiful view, nearly everything in it is tired, used up. Walls not painted in years and years, rugs worn through in some places: the apartment of someone getting old, without the energy to take care. How could they not have noticed? That the apartment was changing, that their mother was. As she wrote, "Presence is only a matter of close attention."

The writer goes to see his mother's first cousin, whom he's located through the family geneologist. Elderly, she's eager for family, to introduce the whole side of the family that her cousin excised from her life at eighteen. Her second husband, perhaps eighty, listens courteously to this talk of tribal feuds fifty years and three thousand miles removed, asks the writer if he ever saw Ted Williams play, then leaves the room to listen to the A's game on radio.

"Your mother," her cousin says. "She was so talented. And she had to excel. She'd say to me, 'You must study more if you want to do better,' expecting I'd want to.

"Your mother's mother, G. She was my aunt. It was so painful to watch her trying to get to see her daughter. You know, your mother and I were once very close—we had the same grandmother, of course. Your mother was scholastically brilliant, but I don't know about her heart. I watched her mother suffer.

"Your grandfather was slight, not tall." ("Short for his age, my father," the writer's mother wrote.) "A terrific guy, a hard worker. He did very well. Your grandmother was tall, heavy-set, outgoing, domineering. Your grandfather tried to heal things after the break. He was a generous man, generous to your father, too. But your mother didn't go to her father's funeral. This was five years after her marriage. To us, it was unconscionable. Also, her break with her mother affected the entire family. None of us ever saw your mother again. It's only my humble opinion, but this was too much.

"Your grandmother had many faults, she just couldn't help herself. She'd do something extraordinarily good, then make a remark that undid it all. She was a very lonely woman, though she kept up a brave front. Nobody really wanted her around. Your father went to see your grandmother when she was dying of cancer of the pancreas. Her hospital was right there near his office, but your mother never came, did she."

Not long after his mother's death:
    *A shopping spree. Nothing expensive, just the consoling act of buying things. Over and over again.

*A sense that the order necessary to survival of the self is barely achieved. That the superego—to pick one set of metaphors—has died, leaving only ego, id.

*What are you going to do now?" friends ask, and he replies, "I'm going on a vision quest." They laugh. He laughs. The writer as Indian on a *rite de passage*. But what, he wonders, what does he mean?

*A conclusion that he and his siblings did a great deal to try to help their mother/worked well together/wore themselves out. Failed to save her.

From the family geneologist, a Xerox of an inscription G. wrote in a book—*Peace of Mind*, by Rabbi Joshua Liebman—she gave in 1946 to her sister's family, "Hoping this will help you to mark out a philosophy of living your life to the full!" The script is large, strong, extroverted, with tremendous sweeps, loops, and curls.

Pictures of the writer's grandmother. From his mother's first cousin, a photo of G. wearing a pinafore at perhaps age ten, in, say, 1890, bangs cut straight across the forehead, hair long in back, a sturdy direct look at the camera. Another photo, G. at perhaps twenty, looking off into middle distance, fabric of her dress gathered in a strong right hand, hair bound up on the top of the head, ear, neck exposed. From the writer's uncle, a picture of G. in forceful middle age, wearing a floral outfit and pumps, in some kind of garden, hand on the neck of a very large flamingo on a stand, an enormous artificial mushroom on the ground beside her. And, from the writer's aunt, a picture of G. in old age. Eyebrows darkened, lipstick, small black hat with veil, skin of the throat yielding to gravity, smile on her face. Looking up at the camera from her soft chair, looking quite small, fading fast.

The writer studies the photos again and again, changes their order, searches for a message, to decipher character, to go past the photos as period pieces or documents of changes in fashion from the late nineteenth to mid-twentieth century. As for the question of family resemblance, the writer calls his mother's cousin. "I would have to say," she concludes, "that no, your mother did not resemble her mother."

"Drastic conditions require drastic remedies," the doctor had said, but now there appears to be nothing more to do. The writer's mother again in an oxygen mask, unconscious, antibiotics suspended—"only prolonging a state that should not be prolonged," the doctor says. And, "her understanding is compromised." More words, phrases: "appropriate supportive care"; "comatose" ; "no turnaround"; "not retrievable medically." The writer and his siblings have formed the habit of listening hard, trying always to decipher the subtext, doctors unable or unwilling to speak without accenting what can be done, what they can do. Limiting discussion to the positive without setting the context of probability, leaving the four of them again and again to fathom the distance between words and tone, explicit versus actual content.

"Has anyone told Mother she's dying?" the writer asks.

The doctor seems discomfitted, replies, "I told her we'd do all we can to keep her comfortable."

Though his mother appears to be in a deep sleep, the writer reads her some of his new stories. Starts to laugh to think of what her line describing the scene would be: *captive audience* . . . Periodically, her eyes open, there's a blank stare for several moments, and then the eyes close again. Are the eye movements connected to his presence? The writer squeezes her hand, asks her to squeeze in response. Nothing.

He puts his manuscript away. "Mother," he begins, "I'm going to tell you a story. Four months ago, in early December, you had a stroke." They've done this before, whenever he felt she needed some chronology in the face of so many operations, repeated stays in ICU, but always before she's been conscious. This time, he again recounts the saga: small periods of recovery, larger relapses, the several operations, the many life-threatening episodes. Finally he reaches the present. "So, Mother, we've determined that this is enough. Sorry for all the mayhem. But that's what I want to say, I promise that now we're getting you out of here."

"One, two, three, testing, testing." Uncle Alfred in 1955, tape recorder running for his mother G. She must have been seventy then, had another five years before she returned to Boston to die.

"I saw one thing in New York that impressed me apropos of the problems of young people today, and that was the play *The Young and the Beautiful.* Born of fine parents, the young heroine, who played her part very well, was nevertheless an unhappy girl of seventeen years. She had everything in life: affection, love, all the comforts and luxuries. She was beautiful besides, so that she had plenty of boyfriends. However, there was something missing. She was sheltered, really had too much. Problems do come when children are too indulged. And that was my reaction to this fine play. I think people who are economically capable of doing well by their children must never say, 'I am going to give them everything I did not have. The best we can give our children are discipline and character. Unfortunately, they must taste life in stark reality. We must suffer, we must be deprived, because after all out of the nest the hard, cold world will not indulge us. And then what happens? We can't take it. End result: neurosis, psychosis, and what have you. Therefore it behooves all intelligent parents to treat their children the way they were treated themselves when they were children. If they just recall that situation they will be very intelligent parents indeed."

For his mother, an ESTIMATED FUNERAL EXPENSE form:
  SERVICES:

Transfer of Deceased	$125.
Procuring Medical & Legal Permits	$50.
CARE OF DECEASED	
Embalming-Refrigeration	$85.
Sanitary Care	$40.
LICENSED PERSONNEL & STAFF	
Arranging, Directing & Supervision of All Details	$175.
FACILITIES	
Facilities & Equipment	$150.
TRANSPORTATION	
Funeral Coach-Service Car	$78.
CEMETERY	
Cremation Fee	$140.
Medical Examiner's Fee	$30.

Rachel, neighbor from down the street when the writer was young. Divorcee with two children, his mother's confidante. "Yes," Rachel says on the phone, "I remember when your grandmother was dying. Your father visited her in the hospital. He'd already been monitoring her condition through his colleagues. And, knowing him, long since he would have been willing to make peace between your mother and grandmother. But on the other hand he would never have tried to make your mother do it. He respected her feelings too much. Anyway, because of your father, that's how your mother knew how she died shouting at the nurse, calling for the supervisor to discipline her. But well before your grandmother died, your mother had concluded that any contact would be inconsistent with her feelings over the years. When your mother told our mutual friend Laura that she would not be going to the hospital, she used that phrase. 'Inconsistent with my feelings over the years.' Laura, a devout Catholic, replied, 'But don't you believe in the grace of God?' "

Late March, the bitter end of winter, cold rain and sleet. Two

weeks after the decision against further invasive tests or surgery. "She's being treated with dignity," the doctor had told
him, which was to say that having been taken off antibiotics
she would soon die.

At ten that night, the nurse calls to say his mother's going
fast. By the time the writer arrives, catheter, urine bag, and
nasal tubes are in the wastebasket, his mother on her back on
the bed, sheets tucked in. Though he's known she was going
to die, though she is better off dead, though her children are
better off having her dead than comatose in some rest home
for years and years, though more than once he'd come into his
mother's hospital room to see her slumped over in the wheel
chair, still the writer cannot help himself. Engulfed in his own
sounds, he hears not crying but howling.

Several minutes later there's a knock on the door, and a
short, heavy, unshaven intern peers into the room, motions
the writer to come out to the corridor.

"Sorry to disturb," the intern says. "Any questions?"

The writer thinks it over. "Yes. What did my mother die of?"

"You mean, did she die of a brainstem stroke? Almost
nobody dies of a brainstem stroke."

"That's what I'm wondering about."

"Really, you'd have to say she died of bad luck. People use
other terms: complications, infections, everything that happens once someone's in a hospital. You know, people assume
doctors know more than they do. Think of it this way: as
doctors we're standing on the beach at the edge of an ocean in
a heavy fog. We know it's a beach, we know it's an ocean, we
know it's a fog, but what's really out there? As far as your
mother was concerned, it was torture in the name of trying to
save her. All those operations. They were long shots, but we
tried. She just had bad luck."

The intern rocks back on his heels. "Let me know if you
need me," he says, and then disappears.

In the wake of their mother's death, the writer's older sister mourning but also gaining strength, stepping in to occupy some of the space now vacated, perhaps intuiting that it is either do that or see it lost entirely. L., the writer's younger sister, of course also now freed in some ways, dealing with relatives and friends with great sympathy and dignity. But then often stumbling with her own grief. Unwilling to imagine letting go of anything from the apartment, for instance, but in the end unable to claim for herself a single piece of the furniture.

The wall mirror. Full length, a fixed center section and two hinged side panels. Writing the contract for the sale of their mother's apartment, they make the mistake of not exempting the mirror from the standard definition of fixtures. When L. finally realizes what's happened—she's clearing out the place, talking to the new owners, is about to take the mirror down— she tries to explain that it has sentimental value, that their mother rehearsed in front of it for years, that it couldn't really be worth very much to anyone else. Unmoved, the new owners insist a deal is a deal.

The writer's friend Sharon. For years they've lived several thousand miles apart. Traveling to Los Angeles and San Francisco, Sharon was visiting him the day his brother called to say their father had died. Eleven years later, back on east coast, he was about to visit her when he learned his mother had suffered a stroke.

Sharon: rich and generous soul, straightforward, true, open. Old friend. And the coincidence of her presence in and around the death of both of his parents.

The writer wonders, is there something more to this, something he should understand?

After his mother's death, a terrible dream that she is very ill, urgently needs help. Is dying.

Laura. Commonwealth accent, bright, wry, direct. "Yes, I did ask your mother if she believed in the grace of God, but not to judge her. It was just a question. More to the point, I remember that your mother once told me that the word best describing her mother was 'adamantine'.

"The torments the generations create. You have to remember, woven into the fabric of your mother's being was her sense of integrity. To give in to this willful woman was to condone her behavior. She just could not do it. She also felt her mother was superficial, fundamentally insecure, desperately seeking the approval of others.

"But think also of the price your mother paid. This tremendous struggle created a great reserve in her. If she'd been free to share her joy with her mother, that would have been quite different. It's not that your mother built a defense but that she used an inner strength not to be wounded in this regard. I have no awe in me," Laura says, "but I respected your mother's needs."

Adamantine. The writer looks it up in his mother's *Webster's*: "Incapable of being broken, dissolved, or penetrated; immoveable . . . Like a diamond in hardness or luster." From Latin, *adamas,* the hardest metal; from Greek, *adamas, a =* not + *daman,* to tame, subdue. Also, in Middle English, confusion with the Latin verb *adamare,* to love, be attached to, hence also meaning 'magnet'.

"Spaced out," he wrote eight months after his mother died. The first writing he'd done since her stroke, after wondering if language, so much part of his inheritance, his mother tongue, had died with the death of this parent, or if words were simply inadequate to the task of living. "Spaced out. Is stroke catching? The writer stutters as he speaks to the young nurse, who laughs. His mother is sitting up in bed, one eye under a patch, the other enlarged. Enormous. 'Sorry,' the writer says to the nurse. 'Forgive me. Sometimes I have trouble with words.' His mother's head slowly rotates to the right, the eye now taking them in. 'You see,' he continues, 'English is actually my second language.' His mother seems to begin to smile. 'That's right, my second language. My first language was desire.' "

A memory of his mother. Once again on the phone with a friend, making a face when one of the children walks by, as if to say she'd like to get off but can't. As if only the needs of the other person keep her on the line.

Ana: very good friend. Parents who survived World War II in Greece; feisty, vibrant brother who died in college. Ana, then, who does not need to try to console, who understands death so very well.

His mother's tuberculosis. Caused, his aunt had said, by G. The sudden termination of his mother's singing career when she was eighteen, possibly forever. Months in Davos taking a rest cure. Weekly pneumothorax. X-ray after X-ray to monitor the disease. Years of a quiet life until the bacilli finally withdrew.

According to a character in Mann's *Magic Mountain*, "Symptoms of disease are nothing but a disguised manifestation of the power of love; and all disease is only love transformed."

From his mother's death certificate:

MARRIED, NEVER MARRIED, WIDOWED, OR DIVORCED
   Widowed
USUAL OCCUPATION
   Author
KIND OF BUSINESS OR INDUSTRY
   Books

Three months after his mother dies, the writer prepares for

minor surgery. The doctor is Danish, a woman in her early forties, articulate, radiating competence, generous, sympathetic. In the preliminary examination, he lies back as instructed, and she takes his head in her hands. "Just relax," she says, though he has absolutely no inclination to resist. That morning, he'd been reading Freud:

"The attributes of life were at some time evoked in inanimate matter . . . In this way the first instinct came into being: the instinct to return to the inanimate state. It was still an easy matter at that time for a living substance to die . . . till decisive external influences altered in such a way as to oblige the still surviving substance to diverge ever more widely from its original course of life . . . before reaching its aim of death. Seen in this light . . . the theoretical importance of the instincts of self-preservation, of self-assertion and of mastery greatly diminishes . . . What we are left with is the fact that the organism wishes to die only in its own fashion . . ."

One last picture of the writer's grandmother. G. at perhaps fifty, at a costume ball, large—hefty—confident, imposing, all rings and bracelets, head held high, not at all afraid of the camera. Quite at home where the event is staged, public. Has in fact perhaps arranged it all, is hostess, patron, trustee. Will be in no hurry to leave such a wonderful party.

Often, the image of his mother lying there those last few days. Quite still, eyes closed, fold of white sheet under her arms. "Comatose" being the doctor's word, apparently meaning "unable to hear, unconscious, beyond reach." The writer's brother nonetheless talking to her for hours each afternoon, determined to elicit some response, to find the way to get through. After all, was their mother not still alive? Still right there. Still within reach. Still breathing in, breathing out. How to know their mother was not hearing every last word? How prove the contrary? How many times had the doctors been no more than half-right? The writer's brother desperate not to abandon their mother for want of the kind of effort she'd always expected—demanded—of her children, of herself.

The writer calls his mother's cousin. The year before, she'd said her older brother would know more than she would about the rift between the writer's grandmother and mother. Her brother was very busy, she said, but would be free soon.

"I'm sorry," she tells the writer now when he calls. "My brother's not well. Alzheimer's, I'm sorry to say. With him, at this point, most of the past is lost. I mean, it's all still in there in his memory, but there's really no access to it. Here and not here, if you see what I mean."

In the words of Wright Morris, "Anything processed by memory is fiction."

Toward the end of his text on autopsy technique, the writer's father speaks of restoration of the body after a post-mortem examination. Incision lines, for example, are closed by stitches, body cavities "dried and cleaned, their external openings (anus, vagina)" plugged with cotton, then "stuffed with sawdust sufficient in amount to restore the external contour of the abdomen."

The writer's father also speaks of autopsy techniques in special conditions—in a private home, or during time of war, for example—and cautions that "No trace of the autopsy be left in the home after the examination has been completed. In homes where fireplaces or coal stoves are available it has been recommended that ground coffee be thrown on a shovel full of burning coals to suppress the odor occasioned by the autopsy. The ingenuity and tact of the pathologist are important in the successful performance of a private autopsy, particularly when relatives or undertakers are present."

The writer is absolutely sure this happened thirty years ago. He was fourteen, the summer after his freshman year of high school. The days were incredibly humid, incredibly hot, and there were frequent thunderstorms with lightning, canopies of the trees opulently thick and green, swaying in the sudden squalls. He and his mother were in the kitchen. There was a red and white checkerboard tablecloth, the old gas range had six burners, there were six chairs at the table. There was a stainless steel bowl on the counter overflowing with grapes, and a bowl of raw peas his mother had just been shelling. She was weeping as she spoke, saying her mother had come back to Boston to die, that she was trying to decide whether or not to go see her. She was telling her son this, but not asking his opinion, not asking to be consoled. Just telling him, though this in itself was extraordinary: neither he nor his siblings ever heard their parents argue, never discussed with their parents or heard them discuss any issue troubling one or the other. Never, except perhaps some years before when their father was ill, before it was clear he'd survive. Perhaps then part of a hard truth was conveyed. But now his mother was speaking about her mother to her son, and he remembers her tears, remembers looking out the kitchen window toward the lilacs, toward the fence, toward the elm trees beyond, yet cannot for the life of him summon up how he replied if at all, how the conversation continued, attenuated, ended. But it was in the kitchen, the lilacs were out the window, he was fourteen, and his mother was weeping.

Thirty years later, thirty years later the writer wonders what, what did his mother fear she'd lost when her mother died?

* * *